MW00962329

A Sharp
Medicine

Dale T. Phillips

Thanks for being a reader.

Dale

Try these other works by Dale T. Phillips

Shadow of the Wendigo (Supernatural Thriller)

The Zack Taylor Mystery Series
A Memory of Grief
A Fall From Grace
A Shadow on the Wall
A Certain Slant of Light

Story Collections
Fables and Fantasies (Fantasy)
More Fables and Fantasies (Fantasy)
Crooked Paths (Mystery/Crime)
More Crooked Paths (Mystery/Crime)
Strange Tales (Magic Realism, Paranormal)
Apocalypse Tango (Science Fiction)
Halls of Horror (Horror)
Jumble Sale (Mixed Genres)
The Big Book of Genre Stories (Different Genres)

Non-fiction Career Help
How to Improve Your Interviewing Skills

With Other Authors
Rogue Wave: Best New England Crime Stories 2015
Red Dawn: Best New England Crime Stories 2016
Windward: Best New England Crime Stories 2017
Insanity Tales
Insanity Tales II: The Sense of Fear

Sign up for my newsletter to get special offers
http://www.daletphillips.com

DEDICATION

To Ernie, and so many others, who went into the darkness and yet came back to share their light with others

ACKNOWLEDGMENTS

It's a tough game to try and outdo yourself with every book, but that's my goal, making each Zack adventure the best it can be.

A hearty thank you to Dave Zeltserman, Ursula Wong, David Daniel, Karen Salemi, and others who took the time and effort to read this work (some multiple times) and offer their suggestions to make it better.

My thanks extend to everyone who helped to make this book possible.

As always, to my wonderful family: Mindy, Bridget, and Erin, for suffering my solitary profession of writing.

To my dear and supportive friends for making things more enjoyable along the path of life.

To all those who have helped teach me to write, through their works.

To all those who read other Zack Taylor mysteries and wanted more.

And to you, dear reader, my thanks, for reading this one.

Feel free to contact me and let me know what you thought of the book and what it's about.

" 'Tis a sharp medicine for all my ills"

—Sir Walter Raleigh, upon seeing the weapon that would soon execute him

(Some sources say the correct spelling is Ralegh, but common usage would make this look like an error.)

Dale T. Phillips

CHAPTER 1

The guy sitting across from me was either a psychiatrist or a psychologist, I didn't know which. What I *did* know was that he was annoying the crap out of me. He looked at me like I was a bug, and spoke to me like I was a dimwitted child. I could handle that, as I'd endured much worse, but he was also saying negative things about Allison's fragile state of mind, when all I wanted to hear was that she was getting better.

He sat behind an ornate desk that looked like it could be rosewood or something equally expensive. He was too well-fed, wearing pricey clothes, and seemed eminently satisfied with himself and his position of authority. When he'd shaken hands with me, his palm and fingers were baby-skin soft, and I doubted he'd ever done a day's hard work in his life. He wasn't so much talking to me like a person as lecturing to me as from a pedestal. The smell of his cologne from across the desk and his gleaming, hairless scalp distracted me while I tried to focus on his message.

His voice was smooth, but had an overbearing, bossy tone, and came out as if he was telling me I owed him money and he was forced to take drastic measures to collect. "Do you understand what I'm saying to you, Mr. Taylor?"

"I think so," I said. "You spent about fifteen minutes telling me, in essence, that Allison is messed up from the shooting."

He frowned, his mouth turning down in disapproval like I was a bad schoolboy. "Post Traumatic Stress Disorder, or PTSD. I was trying to give you an understanding of what it is."

"You mean how the person suffers strong recurring negative emotions, and flashbacks can be triggered by any number of things?"

Now his eyebrows raised. "Well. I see that you *were* listening."

"Yes, I was," I said. "Even the big words. And you might have a better rapport with people if you didn't treat them like they were stupid and beneath you. I know you have that framed degree and all up there on your wall, and this is Maine, but you don't have to assume that everyone who comes in here is a mouth-breathing idiot."

He blinked rapidly, and his lips opened and closed a few times, reminding me of a gulping fish. He broke eye contact completely, looking down at the folder on the desk. He took several deep breaths and composed himself before speaking. "You have a rather confrontational style of conversing, Mr. Taylor."

"Yeah, I hear that a lot. Especially from people who talk down to me. But we're not here about my problems; we're talking about Allison."

"She has suffered an extremely traumatic shock to her system."

I spread my hands. "I got over it. Why is she so messed up? She was only grazed."

His mouth turned down again. "She was almost *killed* in that debacle. The papers called it 'The Shooting Gallery.' "

"That phrase was coined by a scandal sheet hack named Mason Carter, a piece of human garbage with a grudge against me. And just to set the record straight, it was *me* the shooter was trying to kill, not her. Wasn't the first time someone tried to kill me, either. But I'm doing okay."

"Are you really, Mr. Taylor? I think you could benefit from talking to someone."

"No thank you. I'm not getting on your couch so you can pull my brain apart to see what makes me tick."

"With your history of violence, it's unhealthy to bottle your feelings up."

I leaned forward. "Actually, it's absolutely necessary. When I let loose, Doc, people get hurt. And killed. So let's just keep the plug in the jug."

He sat back and studied me. "That's a phrase sometimes used by alcoholics. Would you have some experience with that?"

I shook my head. "Can we please get off the subject of me, and back onto your patient?"

"The stress from the incident caused Miss Chambers to drink herself out of a job, her career in fact, and a settled life. And your relationship is a big part of her situation. Since her alcoholism is now out of control, it is important for me to know if you also have a history of problems with alcohol. I am certain you do."

"Because you read that I was in a prison for a short spell?"

"Because this type of thing is very common in a situation like this."

I ran my hand through my hair. I realized that now *I* was leaning back, and he was leaning forward. We wouldn't get any further unless I gave him what he wanted. So what the hell, open the hood, show him the whole engine. "Fine, yeah, when I was younger, my little brother accidentally shot himself with my pistol. I started drinking to deal with the pain and the guilt, and got pretty bad off, damn near killing myself. A friend brought me here to Maine to kick it cold turkey, and I haven't touched it since."

"I see. And what is it you do for a living?"

"Security Consultant," I said.

"How is that going?"

It wasn't going at all. My second attempt at a legitimate business was another complete failure. With my record, I couldn't get bonded, and without that reassurance, and with all the publicity over the shooting, no one would hire me. I'd tried to bring my friend Theo in as the front man, but he told me there was a "black ceiling." He explained that people were okay with paying him to be a guard, but most folks here wouldn't see a black man as a boss who could guarantee their valuables.

I sighed. "It sucks, to tell you the truth."

"Are you drinking now, or having problems with any substance abuse?"

"No."

He smiled and nodded. "Perhaps not. But you exhibit certain symptoms of what is called a 'dry drunk,'" the hostility being one of the big ones. I believe this is a major part of why Miss Chambers began drinking so heavily."

"You're saying she's drinking because of me?"

"She's doing exactly what you did after a trauma, following a similar path."

"Sounds like I should get her out of here and take her whitewater rafting, then."

"No, no. That might have worked for you, but she's different. She was an emergency room nurse. I imagine she saw a great deal of suffering and death."

"She did until they fired her." I couldn't quite keep the bitterness out of my voice.

"And that added more guilt and stress. You know all about that, don't you?"

"Yeah, I sure as hell do."

"You seem like an intelligent man, Mr. Taylor. You're not going to like what I'm about to say, but I hope you'll understand it and accept it."

I gave him a stone-faced stare.

He went on. "I think that under the circumstances, it's best if you hold off visiting for a time."

"You don't want me to see her?"

"You are one of the triggers of the stress state. She looks at you and sees her own death. She relives that feeling."

I swallowed. He was right. I didn't want to hear this.

"Furthermore, her drinking exacerbates the problem, and due to your history, complicates matters. Your presence fires off a chain of emotions she cannot deal with at present. If we can get her back to a stable state, we can perhaps think about your coming back."

I rubbed the side of my face, suddenly quite weary. "Won't that seem to her like I'm abandoning her in time of need?"

"We will carefully explain things to her, and tell her it was our recommendation, not your idea at all."

"Sounds all wrong."

"It's for the best, I assure you."

I looked at him. I didn't trust him as far as I could throw his fancy desk, but matters of the mind weren't my area of expertise. Allison's problems were more than I could handle, and these people had experience. This clinic that my friend J.C. and I had brought her to was a private place up the coast from Portland, exclusive and pricey. They were supposed to know what they were doing.

"What about J.C.? Can he still come and visit?"

He shook his head. "Given her condition, I'd rather she didn't see anyone from outside for at least four weeks. We'll re-evaluate of course, but for now, she needs time to think of other things than what happened that night. And he is closely tied to you, so better that he refrain from visiting, too."

"How will you help her?"

"She's going to need to focus on other activities. You might think of it as occupational therapy, but it helps to have something to divert one's energy to."

"Painting."

He frowned again. "I beg your pardon?"

"Painting," I repeated. "She's an artist. At least she was until she got into nursing. I could bring her art supplies from home."

He stroked his chin. Probably wished he could grow a beard like Freud's. "That might be helpful. We could certainly give it a try."

I nodded. "Okay then. I'll bring them by later today, and keep away until you give the green light." The conversation seemed to have run its course, so I stood up. "But I'll want to know her progress."

"We'll tell you what we can," he said. "But I would say once again that you too could benefit from our help. You have a guilt complex, combined with resentment and a deep-seated anger. You can't go through life on a continual slow boil."

It's worked for me so far, I thought. Well, until it hadn't.

J.C. was in the waiting area. He bore a strong resemblance to Hemingway, more so now with deep lines of worry etching his brow. "What did they say?"

"I'll tell you on the way," I said. "Not here."

When we were in the car, he turned to me. "So?"

"So our doctor thinks that I'm a bad influence, and doesn't want me, or anyone else visiting her for a few weeks. If we stay away, she can maybe get her head together."

He nodded slowly. "I know you don't agree, but they really are the best at what they do."

"They damn well better be. They have to help her."

"They will."

I looked out the window, seeing the ocean in the distance. Maybe I should get on a boat and sail around the world to forget my problems. "I met with that banker you recommended, and we set up the trust for Allison for when she gets out. She won't have to worry about a job for at least a year or two."

"That's good. It will give her some time. What are you going to do now?"

I felt all the blackness well up inside me. "I don't know," I said. "But I sure as hell want a drink."

CHAPTER 2

J.C. didn't mess around. He knew I meant what I said about wanting a drink, so he took me to an Alcoholics Anonymous meeting. I'd told him it wasn't my thing, but he had the car keys, and he pretty much shanghaied me to some depressing little church basement with a bunch of other people. I didn't wonder that he'd know about a meeting like this, as he seemed to know everyone and everything in Maine.

Most of the people there looked to be in pretty rough shape, with body postures of absolute defeat, and faces that looked like they'd been on the losing end of terrible prizefights. J.C. stuck a paper cup of coffee in my hand. I took a sip to mollify him, but it tasted like battery acid. A number of the others had cups of the vile brew. I wondered if it was some sort of penance.

A man got up and started talking, but I was already tuned out. I figured I could wait through the sad tales until it was time to go, and J.C. would have felt he'd done his due diligence. Then I could get on with wallowing in my misery without his interference.

Some guy in a faded green Army jacket shuffled to the front. He had long hair and a scraggly mustache, and he introduced himself. People greeted him, and he told us all how his marriage had fallen apart and he'd lost his family because all he could do was drink and do drugs when he'd returned from his tour of duty. He had PTSD, he said, and for a long time the damn VA hadn't done much for someone in his condition. The term caught my ear, and I was suddenly paying attention. He told the story of how he felt, and how the drinking and the drugs were the only things that softened the memories enough so he wasn't constantly on edge. He sculpted out in detail the horror of what he was going through, and my mind's eye saw Allison doing something similar. I felt ashamed I hadn't seen what it was, and that I hadn't done enough for her until it was too late. Guilt flooded through me yet again.

I looked at J.C. and practically hissed at him. "You son-of-a-bitch. This wasn't chance. You knew this would get my attention."

He nodded and spoke softly. "Allison's condition isn't really a big secret, you know. I saw her sliding down, too, and figured out what it was. I talked to some people, they pointed me here, and I checked it out. I thought it might help."

I crossed my arms and refused to listen to any more. Several other people got up in turn and spun their tales of woe, of lives ruined, and of hitting rock bottom. I shut it all out.

When I thought we were about done, the first guy went back up front and called out. "Anyone else?"

J.C. walked to the front of the room. What was he doing? I was here, so mission accomplished. He drank fine scotch, and wasn't about to give it up, so why was he speaking?

He cleared his throat. "I'm sorry, but I'm not here for me. My friend is sitting there. Let's call him Duffy."

The people looked at me and murmured a greeting, and I felt my ears going red.

J.C. went on. "He's been sober for a lot of years, but he's having some trouble, and he's dancing on the edge of that big black hole. The woman he loves had a terrible thing happen, she's got PTSD, and she started drinking. We got her into rehab, but Duffy here feels guilty and in pain. He fancies himself a lone wolf, so he's too stupid and stubborn to ever ask for help. Despite that, he helps others, and he's a good person. I don't want to see him destroy himself, and I thought this might do some good. Thank you all for your indulgence." He came and sat back down.

My jaw was hanging open in disbelief.

The man up front was looking at me. "Do you want to say something, Duffy?"

"No, I don't." I got the words out, but just barely, as my throat was thick with emotion. I couldn't just disappear, though I wanted to.

The guy in the Army jacket studied me. "I was like you," he said. His voice was a rasp. "I was too strong to need any help. I could handle the booze. Until it handled me. And everything I had went down the shitter."

I saw a couple of other people nod in agreement.

"I ..." More words wouldn't come out.

"You're a fighter, I can see that," he went on. "Tough guy. But some things are too big. You can't smash your way through this. It's going to eat and eat at you, and never stop. You can hold the pain off for a while, but only by not feeling anything. We're not made to be that way. It just makes us dead inside. I bet you were like that for some time. But now you care for someone else, and she's hurting, and every morning when you wake up, you feel like you swallowed razor blades. And it's just gonna get worse as the day goes on. You'll want something, need something, to take the edge off that massive pressure that's always there. One slip, and that makes the next one easier, then the next. You did booze before, and you'll go back to it. Some of us went with other shit, too. Me, I got into heroin when I wasn't drinking. Turned into a fuckin' junkie, 'cause it was the only other thing that made the bad shit go away for a while."

The guy looked around and shrugged. "Even thought about just ending it all, putting a hot load into the needle and takin' the ride. Figured what the hell, I wasn't doin' anybody much good. Better to end the pain, get it over with."

"What happened, Sam?" The emcee was watching us. No one else spoke.

"My kids. I'd already blown it with the old lady. She'd given up on me, but I wanted to see my kids again. So I held off. Then came this new government program. So they stopped putting me in jail and got me into treatment instead. Kickin' the shit sucked, I can tell you. But I did it, with help, and I've been clean and sober for seven months and four days. I do a meeting a day now, sometimes two. And I'm damn glad to see each day come in, even with all the shit behind me."

"What about your kids?" The woman who was asking had tears in her eyes.

"The old lady took off with them. I don't know where they are, but I'd like to find them some day and tell them how sorry I am."

A chair scraped, and someone coughed. Sam turned back to me. "Your lady's gonna need you, son. She's got a battle of her own to fight, and if you take the booze route, it just might take her down with it. So you'll have to get help. If we're not it, fine, but you're gonna need to talk to someone."

I couldn't look at anything but my hands in my lap.

"You may not be ready now, but you'll need to do it soon. You'll have to make your choice, booze or help. One will kill you and your lady, the other might save you both. Your call."

CHAPTER 3

That night, I didn't even try to get to sleep. It was as if my head was tightly wrapped in barbed wire. I paced around, constantly wiping my mouth. My hands kept closing into fists, and I wanted to hit something and make it hurt like I was hurting.

I was in Allison's big old Victorian house in Portland's West End, and everything I saw was a reproach. No matter where I looked, I was reminded of how I'd put her in danger and why it was that she wasn't here. She'd had a couple of nurses paying rent to stay in the upstairs, but they'd left when her drinking caused problems. That was a week before the hospital had fired her. Her life had turned to shit, and it was my fault for taking her to that art gallery where the shooting had occurred.

Good thing I'd long since thrown out all the booze in the house. My mouth was dry, and I wanted something so bad, I could almost conjure a bottle in front of me. Drinking at least gives you something to do. You sit and suck down the poison until your brain drowns. The trouble is, that becomes the be-all and end-all, and I'd been shamed out of that, at least for the time being. But I was shaking and needed something.

My other drug, just as powerful and just as destructive, was violence. I was a kick-boxer and had done some other martial arts, and I loved getting into a good fight. I looked at the clock, and it was midnight. The Witching Hour. Anytime you go out after that, you're sure to find trouble. I grabbed my car keys and headed for the door.

I thought about where to go to unleash the beast. Ollie Southern, the guy who'd tried to kill me in the gallery and caused all of these problems, was a former leader of a biker gang. I'd first met him in a dive biker bar in Lewiston, only a half hour away. It would still be open, and there might be some of his old gang there. A few members of that crew had previously tried to beat me to death, and were doing time because of it. Stupid me decided that the bar was as good place as any to try to get hurt.

I headed up the turnpike toward Lewiston, feeling the edges of my world crackle and burn to black. I wanted blood, and didn't really care if mine was shed in the process. I squeezed the steering wheel, anticipating the moves, savoring the bloodlust welling up inside me.

Most of Lewiston was off the streets, the only ones left being night people, those who knew only darkness and lived apart from normal folk: a couple of hookers, those looking to buy or sell drugs, and the rest like me, looking for worse trouble.

The bar was lit with neon signs, and I gave a grim smile to see a pair of motorcycles out front. I parked with the car pointing in the direction of escape, in case I needed to make a fast getaway.

I stood outside, hearing music from within, and seeing the darkened windows of the houses around. I wondered if anyone was looking down at me, and what they would think of the man doing strange stretches in the night air. I breathed full and deep, and walked over to the front door.

Inside was as dim and depressing as when I'd been there before. There were no women, just a pair of guys playing pool and three more sitting around drinking longneck beers. Two of the guys had the official jacket of Ollie's gang. Everyone stopped what they were doing to look at me.

I pointed at the two with the gang jackets. "You know who I am. I'm the guy who got Ollie Southern killed and your brothers put in jail. If you want to do something about that, I'll be outside knocking over your shitty bikes."

I went back outside, feeling the rush of imminent mayhem.

CHAPTER 4

It took two days before most of the swelling had gone away and I could move normally. My face was puffy and my body was still sore, and I had an ugly slash across one ear. But I hadn't needed stitches or any casts, and I was still alive. Too bad.

I couldn't do this anymore; I had nothing left. So I called J.C. and finally asked for some help. I'd been fighting off ghosts from my past for too long, and the new problems added on were too much. I'd spent years just getting by and forming no emotional attachments. When my friend Ben was killed I'd come to Maine to find the truth, and almost been killed myself in the process. Then I'd broken all my rules about keeping my emotions in check and fell in love. But that had ruined her life by pulling her into my sphere of violence. Now I was alone again with time to dwell on little more than memories and regrets.

This shrink, Sanders, was different from the one at the rehab center. Sanders didn't talk down to me, was trim and fit, and he gave off an air of professionalism without overbearing authority.

There was no couch in his office, just a comfy, overstuffed chair. And he didn't hide behind an expensive desk, but sat in a chair beside me. He had a smile that didn't seem forced, despite my roughed-up appearance. But his eyes were sharp and he didn't look like a pushover.

"So what's up, Mr. Taylor?" His voice was deep and soothing, like a TV announcer's. "What brings you in to see me? Apart from a car, that is." He gave a slight smile at his own joke.

I didn't know how else to say it. "I hurt people. And now because of it, someone I love is in trouble, and it's my fault."

"Is that what all this is about?" He circled his pen in the air to indicate my battered face.

"This is my stupid way of dealing with it. Collateral damage. But I can't do this anymore."

"Would you like to tell me about it?"

Once I got started, it all came pouring out. It was a good thing we'd arranged for a two-hour consult, twice the normal session, because it took that long to fill the good doctor in on my sad and sordid past, and what had happened since I came to Maine. I finished off with recent events, including why Allison was in rehab, and why I looked like a mugging victim.

He let me speak and didn't comment as I told my tale, but I did see his eyebrows go up a few times when I described some of the messier parts. I suspected J.C. had prepared him, otherwise I might have sounded like someone who made things up.

At least he looked like he believed me. Hell, with my face all marked the way it was, who wouldn't think that I was a violent guy with troubles? And maybe he'd seen the stories in the papers about some of the criminal entanglements I'd encountered.

He paused at the end of my tale of woe, looking thoughtful. I had to admit that spilling it all out like that did make me feel a little lighter. Holding on to a load of guilt takes a lot of effort, like hauling around a sack of stones.

"So what do you think, Doc? Any hope for me?"

He smiled. "There's always hope, even for the worst of us."

"Getting a little close to religion, aren't you?"

"Not a religious man?"

"Any vestige I had went out when my little brother died."

"You know," he said quietly, "our past does not have to dictate our future. You make the next choice, and the one after that, and so on. They can be choices radically different from what you've previously done. When I say hope, I mean it. You stopped drinking at one point, and managed to keep from doing that for years, even while working in a bar. That takes a lot of internal fortitude. You were in prison, but got out intact, and even now seek to be a better person. You want to help others, yet you blame yourself for every bad outcome. That's something we can work on. Every terrible thing is not your fault, even though you feel you're the one who sets things in motion."

"This latest thing, though—"

"Was an outside agent. You know how many people have lost someone, in say a car accident, and blamed themselves for the rest of their lives? *'If only I'd gone alone. If I hadn't taken that road. If I'd stopped to tie my shoes.'* On and on, they find a hundred things they could have done to prevent the tragedy from occurring. And you know what? You can't play that game. Shit happens, and we're arrogant enough to think we could have averted disaster if we'd done something different. Our nature lets us torture ourselves because we don't have godlike powers, because life drops a load on us."

"What if we should have known better?"

"Let me ask you something. Did you ever forgive anyone for doing something they shouldn't have?"

"Well, yeah, sure."

"So why can't you forgive yourself?"

I blinked. I'd once said something very much like this to a woman I'd taken from an abusive situation, someone who thought she somehow deserved all the bad shit that had come her way.

"Because I keep doing things that get people hurt."

"You cannot control the actions of those who hurt others, and you can't make them stop trying to strike out at innocent people. They'll continue to do that until they're stopped. From what you've said, you've had a hand in ending the hurting careers of some pretty bad people and even saved a few others. But you're not God or Superman. Life's going to happen, whether you're there or not."

I breathed out and ran my hands through my hair, my head down. "I see ghosts sometimes."

"As do a lot of people. Man, you want folks who see ghosts, talk to some servicemen who were in any of our last few wars. You've never pulled the trigger on women and children, have you? Seen a pile of corpses of people who've died for no good reason?"

"No, nothing like that."

"Then count your blessings. All violence leaves a stain on a person. Whether it's you doing it to someone else, or having it done to you, it leaves scars. I'm not saying your problems don't matter, but I would say you don't have near as far to go down the road of forgiveness as some. Do you think they deserve a chance to go on?"

I thought of the ex-soldier from the AA meeting, and wondered what he'd seen that drove him to want to scrub his brain of past images. Things that made him drink away his family, and then turn to shooting junk into his veins. "Yeah."

"Okay, then. We've got some work to do. You work on getting through the rest of the day without taking a drink or fighting someone. Can you do that?"

"Yeah."

"Good. Then do the same again tomorrow. Come see me the day after that, Saturday at two."

"Okay."

He sat back. "You seem pretty subdued now. Calmer. Notice your leg isn't jittering, like it was when you came in?"

"You're right. Guess I've got a lot to think about."

"Yes, you do. I take it you're not the AA type, and you said you weren't religious. Shame, because either of those can be a big help. Do you have anybody you can call when things get really bad in the meantime?"

"J.C."

"He knows a lot about forgiveness and pain. It's good to have him in your corner. That means something."

"How do I keep my mind in the right place? It used to be my martial arts practice, but I'm too angry to even do that anymore."

"It would help if you had something external to focus on."

"You mean like someone else's problems?"

He smiled. "How about something more positive?"

I didn't respond. I couldn't think of anything positive that was strong enough to distract me. That was the issue.

Dale T. Phillips

CHAPTER 5

When J.C. said he wanted me to meet someone, I almost said no. After his setting me up with an AA meeting and a psychiatrist, I wasn't sure how much more help from him I could take.

We met at a restaurant in Lewiston that billed itself as Polynesian, which puzzled me, because J.C. loved good food and drink, and knew all the best places for dining. There were dozens of them in Portland that didn't require a thirty-minute drive. Because of the publicity of the news stories detailing my brushes with the law, and the frenzy over the shooting, I'd taken to wearing Red Sox caps and dark sunglasses, feeling like a celebrity stalked by paparazzi. I now understood what they lived like, fearful of being recognized and hounded every time they left the sanctity of their home.

J.C. waved his hand at the man sitting next to him. "Zack Taylor, meet Bob Murrow."

Bob stood up to shake hands. He topped out at five-six, over four inches shorter than me, thin, late fifties. He wore glasses and had a worried air. His handshake was firm, though. No calluses, so he didn't do heavy manual work with his hands. He looked more the scholarly type anyway.

I noted that J.C. didn't have his usual tumbler of scotch in front of him, and they'd been seated when I arrived. For a guy who looked a lot like Hemingway and sometimes drank to match, this was quite the anomaly. I looked around at the décor. "What's with this place? Don't tell me they have a particular dish you can't get anywhere else."

J.C. gave me a look like I was an idiot.

The light dawned. "Ah. You won't run into anyone you know here. And I'm guessing the food is probably as bad as the ambiance."

"We're not eating. I told them to just leave us bc," J.C. nodded. "Bob here runs a weekly newspaper on the coast."

The anger ran ahead of my thought processes. I'd been hounded by so many people from the papers that I lumped them as a group and hated them all. Except for J.C. himself, who worked for the *Maine Times*.

"A *newspaper*? What were you thinking?" I was about to get a good head of steam, but J.C. cut me off.

"This isn't about you. He's not here to detail your messes."

"Then what?"

"One of my reporters is missing," Bob's voice was quiet, and the lines on his face seemed to deepen. "A young woman."

I closed my mouth, which had once more been about to run without my brain connected. I took a deep breath and pushed the anger back down so I could think. This just beat all.

Bob pushed a photograph across the table. "Georgette Chapelle. Twenty-six. Worked for me for almost a year. Did good work, wanted more, wanted bigger. Always looking for the story that would be her break, the next step up."

I frowned. "She looks familiar. Was she on TV or something?"

"No. You might have seen her for one of your court cases."

"Yeah, that's it. She tagged me outside the courthouse once, tried asking me a couple of questions, and I played stupid."

"Easy for you," J.C. piped in. I shot him a dirty look.

Bob nodded. "She'd read some of that Mason Carter crap, wanted to know if there was anything to it. So she went to Portland, took a look around. Decided there was too much competition. Every other reporter in the state was there. She liked the stories no one else was doing."

"How long has she been gone?"

"Don't know for sure. At least a few days."

"Was she working some new story?"

"She was *always* working on a new story. Several."

"You think one of those might have got her into trouble?"

"I do. The scary stories have the most appeal. She might have got in over her head."

"Have you talked to the police?"

Bob took off his glasses and polished them with a napkin before answering. "No. I was getting worried, so I stopped by her apartment. The landlady said she'd left a note."

Bob pushed over a sheet of paper with some writing on it.

Hi- I'll be away for awhile. Everythings okay, if you could keep an eye on my place. Thanks, G

"That her handwriting?"

"Yes," said Bob. "But. She would never use *'awhile,'* and there's no apostrophe on *everythings.*" He pointed them out.

"That mean something?"

"She was strict with grammar. It means she wrote this under duress, hoping I'd see it and know she needed help."

"And no police, because …"

Because they'd think I was a crackpot wasting their time. A note in her handwriting, case closed. Have you ever worked with the police?"

I grimaced. "Once or twice, yeah."

"Then you know. They'd take my name and info and go back to doing whatever."

I looked at J.C., who spread his hands. "He called me, and I naturally thought of you."

I tapped the paper. "You're sure there's something wrong here."

"I'm a newspaperman, have been for over twenty years. My gut instinct is great. And she's missing."

"No way she went undercover for a story?"

"Not without getting word to me first, in some way. A note for her landlady? Not her style. The landlady's a snoop, anyway."

"You see if there was anything missing in her place?"

"The landlady is also a good watchdog, and won't let anyone in."

"Did the landlady see her leave?"

"Said no, and they didn't speak. Just the note."

I looked at the paper. "What about her family?"

"Gone. No brothers or sisters, her mom and dad passed away. She's had to make it on her own through some tough times, and that shaped her as a reporter. Spunky kid. Likeable. Didn't mind breaking the rules to get the story. She wanted to use this photo for her own byline."

I looked closer at the photo. Nice young woman, smiling, with a small crease in her brow that showed she had a serious streak. Shortish hair, brown, looked like she could have still been in college.

I pushed it back. "Sorry, but I've kind of got my own problems right now."

J.C. slapped his hand down on the table. His voice was sharp. "You don't get to say no on this."

"Excuse me?"

He didn't back down from my glare. "What, you're going to sit around feeling sorry for yourself? Sulk in your tent, like Achilles?

Goddamnit, you're only effective when you're doing something like this."

"Thanks a lot."

"You know what I mean. There's nothing you love more than turning over rocks, looking for answers."

"I love Allison more."

"And you can't even see her. So enough wallowing in your own misery. Make yourself useful and find this woman."

I looked at him, wanting to unload. But he was right, damn his eyes. I let my breath out and sagged in my seat. I tried one more time. "People get hurt when I do this kind of thing."

"People get hurt regardless. Look at the picture. Who else can find her?"

Murrow had remained silent through our exchange, looking from one of us to the other.

I shook my head, but looked at the photo. I picked it up and studied it. "Can I keep this? I may need to show it around."

"Sure," said Murrow. "Here's her address, number seventeen. Landlady is Mrs. Boudreau, apartment directly across. And here's my number. Call day or night, whatever you need."

"Okay. I'll see what I can do."

Bob ducked his head as if embarrassed. "About paying you. I can get a little now, and—"

I waved my hand. "Don't worry about it."

"But—"

J.C. put a hand on Bob's arm. "It's covered, Bob. And despite what I say about this guy, if anyone can find her, it's him."

I wished I'd been as sure as J.C.

CHAPTER 6

The missing woman was another stone on my chest. I hadn't wanted to crush Bob's hopes right from the start, but I wasn't likely to find anything. If she'd been taken by someone, it meant she was, in all probability, dead. The statistics on missing young females were depressing and grim.

Bob Murrow would probably blame himself to the end of his days, all for nothing. Thus is human suffering born. Allison had taken to the bottle to deal with the darkness I'd dragged her to, and I was tempted to join her and go back down that road myself. The weight of the many terrible things I'd done was pressing down on me, and I wanted was a release from it. The black void was calling to me, and sounded better all the time.

To distract myself, and because I'd promised to look into her disappearance, I drove to the address of Georgette Chappelle, just across the river from Lewiston, in an apartment complex in the town of Auburn. Number seventeen was indeed directly across from the landlady. She was already peering out the window at me, ever-vigilant watchdog that she was. I smiled and went to knock on her door.

The plump, middle-aged woman had her arms crossed, and her face showed obvious displeasure, the corners of her mouth turned down, the eyes hard and unforgiving.

I smiled wider. "Mrs. Boudreau?"

A tiny dog barked in rapid-fire bursts, and she shushed it. "Roland, be quiet." He didn't stop.

I figured her for French-Canadian, so I tried a shot at heritage pride. "You named him Roland? For Charlemagne's hero?"

She frowned at me even more. "No, for my ex-husband. He was a pain in the ass, too. What do you want?"

I kept the smile on. "I understand you got a notc from Georgette, in number seventeen."

"When is this going to stop?" She said. "You're all driving Roland crazy, and me, too. Why don't you just go away?"

All? "Was there someone else here besides Mr. Murrow?"

"Roland, will you *shut up.*" She turned back to me. "You mean the cops, who came by yesterday, fiddling at the door? I came out and asked them what they thought they were doing. One took out a badge, and said they were the police. Said they had a noise complaint, wanted to check the place out. I told them to come back with a warrant, or take a hike. So they hiked."

"Were they dressed in police uniforms?"

"No, they both wore a suit and tie. Like on *Law and Order.*"

"Anything about them strike you as strange?"

She bent down and scooped up the little dog, who quivered in her arms. At least he finally quieted down, but he looked ready to leap for my throat. "Not really. They looked embarrassed at first, then got mad when I wouldn't let them in. Why?"

"Well, a simple noise complaint is usually handled by uniformed officers, and these sound like they were detectives, who don't normally take calls like that. Do you know who called in the complaint?"

"They didn't say." She eyed me, "And you didn't say who *you* were, with your banged-up face."

"Dave Johnson," I said, sticking out my hand. She didn't take it, and Roland eyed my hand like he wanted a bite of it. I came up with an instant lie. "We were supposed to play tennis today. I got this from getting smacked with a racket." I was no more a tennis player than she was a prima ballerina, but it sounded good.

She frowned. "I didn't know she played tennis."

"I was teaching her."

"You're not dressed for it."

"Oh, we change at the club."

She sniffed. "You some rich man, don't have a job to go to?"

Nothing like a little class resentment. "I work nights. She's got odd hours sometimes, too, so we agreed on today. I called her office and was told she'd left a note?"

"On her door last night, when I got home. I gave it to her boss when he came by this morning. I'd hoped that would be the end of it, but apparently not."

"You weren't here last night?"

She flushed, a little smile finally appearing on her face, and yet it didn't crack. "I won a contest. Darndest thing. Woman came to my door about four o'clock, said I'd won dinner for two anywhere in town, for that night. I called Marie, and we went out for a lovely meal. Had to leave poor Roland here alone, and Susan next door said he barked the whole time."

I'll bet he did, I thought.

"So there was no note when you left, but it was there when you got back?"

The suspicious look was back. "That's right."

"And you didn't see her car at any point?"

She shook her head. "You ask a lot of questions for a man who plays tennis."

I nodded. "Sorry. It's just strange, that's all. She was good about keeping appointments, and she didn't call to cancel, and then you say the police came by."

"Well, she left a note."

"But nobody saw her car while she was supposedly here."

"Roland was barking the whole time I was out. So somebody was in her place. She probably just came by to get something. Maybe she was in a hurry."

I knew better than to ask to get into the apartment. She already had me pegged as a suspicious character, and that would have made her call the cops.

"Well, I guess I'm out of luck, then."

"I'd say you are. Maybe you can catch her at church."

"On Sunday?"

"Tonight. She started going to that big new one, Church of the Redeemer." She gave me the address. "They have a Friday night service, and Bingo on Thursdays."

"Thanks. I'll swing by there, see if she shows up."

"You can tell her I'm tired of all the people coming around to see her. She should do something about that."

"I will. Say, what contest did you win? Maybe I can enter, get a nice dinner?"

"The *Sun*." Seeing my lack of comprehension, she went on. "The Lewiston Daily Sun, the newspaper."

"How did you enter?"

"I didn't. How strange is that?"

Very strange, I thought.

CHAPTER 7

The church that the snoopy landlady had mentioned was about a twenty-minute drive from Portland, and I got there in time for their Friday night service. The parking lot was an adjacent field, and several teens in orange vests were directing people where to go.

I gazed at the church, a new, spacious building, which looked like a lot of money had gone into it. Apparently the God business paid well. There was a huge sign advertising the Thursday Night Bingo, so maybe that was where the funds came from.

Taking a seat in a pew in the back, I did a quick count and ballparked the attendance at about two hundred or so. A choir in robes started singing, and the crowd quieted down. The preacher got up after they'd finished, and the play began. He had a good voice, and drew your attention, if you weren't like me and looking around at everybody else. He didn't do the old time fire and brimstone exhortations, but he kept it interesting enough, judging from the many who nodded in agreement. The choir got back up and sang some more.

Inevitably the collection plates came out, and young men started passing along the ends of the pews, distributing to each row. I didn't like the marriage of money and religion, whatever the church. I'd been to the Vatican in my travels, and saw priests after a service transporting huge baskets of money from the donations, and nuns hawking overpriced religious souvenirs in the gift shop. Many of the churchgoers there were poor, and I thought they could have used it more than the church coffers, already stuffed with billions. This church seemed to be doing rather well, too, and in this part of Maine, most people didn't have a lot of cash to spare.

After the service, the crowd got up and slowly filed out, as I hung back. The preacher was by the door, greeting everyone as they left. I had the picture of Georgette, and wanted to see if he recognized her. As I approached, he put his hand out to touch my shoulder, but he saw the look I flashed and withdrew it. His smile faltered for only a moment.

"You're new here." His eyes were brown and he gazed into my face as if I were the most important person in the world. "Welcome. I'm Caleb Martin."

"Heard a few things, wanted to check it out."

"I hope we met your expectations."

I shrugged.

"What is it you were looking for?"

"Not a Bingo game."

He laughed. "You disapprove of our offering entertainment along with fundraising?"

"We still talking about the Bingo? Or the sermon?"

His eyebrows went up. Some men might have been offended at my deliberate needling, but he took it in stride. I liked him for it.

He waved a hand. "None of this is what matters. What truly matters is your relationship with God."

"Yeah, well, he and I haven't been on speaking terms for a long time."

His eyes focused on my face. "I'd like to hear why."

Most people didn't really want the truth, no matter what they said. From time to time I spit it out, just to shock them out of their complacency, and I felt the urge now. "He killed my little brother. I offered the usual bargain, that I'd be a good person if he didn't, but he wasn't interested in the deal, or was away on business, as Tom Waits puts it. So my brother died, and I'm a bad person."

Someone approached us from outside, but the preacher shooed them away. Another point in his favor. "You're in a lot of pain."

"Yeah, well, that's life, right?"

"Sometimes it is. I get where you're coming from. My wife was taken from me two years ago. I would have offered the same deal, with the same results, but I didn't get the chance. And I felt guilty, and I didn't know how I could go on without her. And I wanted to kill myself."

My mouth was dry. "What did you do?"

"I got a gun. I spent a lot of time staring at it, ready to use it to end my pain, but I didn't. I needed to be there for others. For my son, and for this community. Now my son has problems, and I feel guilty about that as well. I've never stopped believing I should have done things differently, and never stopped being resentful about what happened."

"What's all this for, then?" I waved my hand to indicate the church.

"Helping others. I have to live with the things I did. God forgives all, but I haven't forgiven myself. You haven't forgiven yourself, either, I can tell. What I do is work off my debt by seeing that the pain of others is lessened. I bring them to the light, even if I can't reach it myself. So my personal suffering has meaning, since it reminds me how others are suffering. I can do something about that, so I can go on."

My eyes stung, and I felt like I'd been hit with an electric shock. Damn, he'd reached me, and I wanted to change the subject before I broke down. The part about helping others touched a corner of my mind, and I remembered my purpose in coming here. I took out the picture of Georgette. "Have you seen this woman?"

He eyed me for a moment, and studied the photo. "Yes, she came by twice that I saw. Strangers stand out, even with this many people. She skittered away each time I tried to approach. Are you here because of her?"

I nodded.

He smiled. "You may not want to think so, but maybe God sent you, then."

I had my doubts, but kept them to myself.

"She looked curious, but not in pain, like you. People come for a variety of reasons. And we do what we can for them, no matter what they've done, or why they came." He held out his hand, and I shook it. "You didn't tell me your name."

"Zack Taylor."

"Zack, I'd like it if you came back. How about Sunday? We get a celebrity. Helen Schiller, who's running for Senator."

"I'm not much on politicians, but I'll come back."

I would certainly be back. I didn't know what Georgette had been looking for, but for me, this had been like being back with the psychiatrist, and I hadn't even had to pay him two hundred dollars.

CHAPTER 8

Straight from a church to breaking and entering. Was it a sin to sneak into a place if you were only trying to help, and weren't stealing anything? I didn't know, but I was willing to commit another sin in the interests of doing good. But it *was* against the law, so I had to be careful. The landlady was in, was snoopy, and had met me and talked about the apartment. She could pull me from a lineup, if it came to that. And I'd go back to jail. So stealth was of utmost importance.

In my bad old days, I'd worked for a short time with some guys who knew a thing or two about breaking into places. Prison had introduced me to a few more amateur locksmiths, so I had a set of basic skills that could defeat cheap, simple locks. Places like this didn't spend much on expensive deterrents like good locks, figuring the proximity of others was enough to keep most of the riffraff out.

Feeling far too criminal, I put on a pair of latex gloves so as not to leave fingerprints. In the darkness at the back of the place, I used my Swiss Army knife to jigger with the lock. It opened after a couple of minutes. Inside, there were no lights on, but I called out, just in case anyone was actually still there. I locked the door behind me and flicked my penlight on, careful to point the beam downward so it wouldn't show through the windows.

All was silent and stuffy, with that empty feeling places get when no one has been there for a time. I checked the refrigerator, sniffing the milk, and pulled away quickly from the sour smell. There were no bowls out for pet food, or sign of anything like a fishbowl or birdcage, so I wouldn't have to deal with an abandoned pet. I did a quick pass through to confirm there was no one living or dead to encounter.

The place was simple and unpretentious, if rather messy. No home computer, so I guess she used the oncs at work, or had a laptop she'd taken with her. Too bad, as that might have had some clues. I played the messages on the answering machine. There were five from Bob Murrow, two sales calls, and one from a dentist's office about a missed appointment today. Not a good sign.

I checked the drawers in the kitchen and living room area, but they yielded nothing of interest, apart from a book of matches from a Portland strip club, with the name Carol inked on the inside cover. I found that tidbit interesting and took it for future reference. No car keys turned up, so maybe she'd been on the move when she disappeared. I'd get my friend Theo to run her name, get the license plate number, and see if her car had been found.

There was a variety of women's care products in the bathroom, no men's, and her toothbrush was still there. As far as I could tell, it looked like she'd intended to return. No prescription medicines were present in the mirrored cubby over the sink.

The bedroom drawers showed that the clothes had been pulled out and stuffed back in. Same with the closet. I put that with the disorder of everything and confirmed that the place had been searched already. They hadn't just ripped the place apart; that would be obvious. They'd made the effort so that if you didn't know, you couldn't say for sure it had been tossed.

Sonofabitch. Likely it was the guys posing as cops who'd shown up before. Flash any kind of badge at people, and they usually accept it as genuine. And I'd bet money that they'd got someone to show up with the "contest prize," which was nothing more than a way to get the nosy landlady out of her place for a couple of hours while they went through this apartment. That told me I was dealing with someone smarter and with more resources than the common run of crooks.

So what were they looking for? There were papers in a disordered pile on the counter, and I went through each of those. Nothing, though I'd hoped at least for a phone bill so I could see who she'd been in contact with.

I did a more careful check, now looking at the undersides of drawers, feeling around for stuff hidden in odd places. I didn't know just how thorough our previous visitors had been, so I took the time and made a clean sweep. I came up with a double handful of nothing.

Barking erupted from right outside the window, and I saw a shape. I turned off the penlight and froze in place as a woman tapped on the glass and called out. "Is someone in there?"

I recognized the voice of Mrs. Boudreau, the landlady. Dammit. She was at the back, where I'd come in. If I bolted out the front, facing the brightly-lit courtyard, someone was sure to see me, especially with the racket that damn little dog was making. I was trapped.

"Is someone in there? You'd better come out, or I'm calling the police."

I ran through my options, none of them good, as all of them pointed toward jail. There was no cover story she'd buy. Maybe I could hide my head while I ran, and maybe she wouldn't recognize me. But if they questioned Bob Murrow, who had given her his name, he might tell them about me.

Murrow. I had his number. I kept out of sight and inched toward the phone. Curling my hand around the penlight, I shielded the beam to read the number off the card he'd given me. I dialed the phone, praying. Maybe the preacher had had an influence on me, or like foxholes, maybe there were no atheists during break-ins.

Mrs. Boudreau continued to rap the glass and call out, and even rattle the doorknob, while the dog never let up with the barking. His agitation was likely the reason she thought someone was in here.

"Yes?" A male voice answered the phone on the other end.

"Murrow?"

"Yes. Who is this?"

"Zack Taylor, the guy looking for Georgette."

"Have you found anything?"

"Not yet, but I need your help. I'm in her apartment, and the landlady is outside, so I can't leave. If she recognizes me, or the cops get here, I'm screwed."

"I don't understand. You broke into Georgette's place?"

"Yes, but someone beat me to it. No time to talk now. Come and distract the landlady so I can get out of here. She's around back. Tell her you heard there were some cops trying to get in. Ask her about that."

"I'm not sure—"

"If you don't come and get her out of here so I can leave, no one is going to hunt for your reporter."

"Fine. I'll be over there in ten minutes."

"Make it five."

Time stretched out to an eternity. The landlady kept tapping the glass and peering in. I hoped her annoyance at the fake cops and the parade of people would be enough for her to hold off calling the police for a few minutes. Twice I was sure I heard sirens, and my sphincter clenched in response. If I saw a cop car in front, I'd bolt out the back anyway, even if I had to knock over the landlady.

Headlights appeared as a car screeched to a stop in the courtyard. Murrow exited his car and called out. "Mrs. Boudreau?"

He met her by the side of the place, the dog continuing to yap. She tried to shush it now, and moved more toward the front. I slowly unlocked the back, slipped out and relocked it, and started to run.

The dog must have leapt out of her arms, for it came charging around the corner at me, barking all the while. I knew she'd be hot on his heels, and I ran for my life, Roland chasing me like a tiny avenging hellhound.

Dale T. Phillips

CHAPTER 9

I was down in a dark well, and a booming sound filled the space as I touched the wet, smooth stones. I spun around and around, but couldn't find a way out. It took a moment to realize I was dreaming, and the thudding sound I heard was someone pounding at the front door. I got out of bed and went downstairs.

I yanked open the door to confront a red-faced Warren Fielding. When a Treasury agent wakes you, it's already a bad start to the day. "What the hell do you want?"

"What were you doing last night at the Church of the Redeemer?"

I looked at him in stupefaction, my brain slow to comprehend. "You're having me followed?" I felt anger surging, and I'd barely woken up.

"Don't flatter yourself. You're not that important."

"Then what? How the hell did you know I was there? Oh." It flashed in my head. "You're investigating them. For crying out loud. I can't believe this."

"So what were you there for?"

"You woke me. If you want me to be civil, you're going to have to wait for coffee. Want some?"

"What I *want* is for you to keep the fuck away from my investigations."

"Don't yell. You'll wake the neighbors." I put a finger to my lips.

"*Fuck* the neighbors."

"I don't think they'd like that. Or maybe they would. Anyway, I'm making coffee. You can stand out here until I'm done, or you can come in."

I retreated, and he gave in and followed. I went to the kitchen and started a pot of strong brew.

"Look," I said, "I don't know anything about any financials. I went there looking for a missing reporter. She went there, and I don't know why."

"A *reporter*? *Shit, shit, double goddamn shit!*"

"I take it you're not pleased."

He put his head in his hands. "I think you've been put here by the Fates to fuck up my career at every step."

"You've got a job. I've got a young woman who's gone missing. I don't know if they had anything to do with it, but I'll be checking. Sorry if that bounces up against your case. Maybe you should give me a list of places and people you're investigating, so I can stay away."

"I might as well retire now," he said.

"What about the names I gave you in the art forgeries? Can't you build a good case from those?"

His mouth turned tight at the mention. "We're working on it."

I stayed silent, knowing it could take years to prepare a solid indictment at the glacial bureaucratic pace.

"Listen," he said, his face dark, "I know what you think about us. Fuck you, I don't care. I have been stuck up here in exile the past three years, working my ass off, trying to get my goddamn career back. Like the oil business, you drill a couple of dry holes, you go bust. And I had three cases go away before this, just disappear up in smoke, with nothing to show. So they sent me here, out to pasture. Fucking Maine, the seat of all things financial, right? Then I finally get a good trail on that Harada guy, and maybe I can actually build something, with a connection to the Holloways, the whole Yellow Brick Road that leads to bringing them all down. Then *bam*, Harada's whacked when you get involved, and I'm back trying to track money transactions. I get closer on the Holloways, and then *bam*, one of *them* gets whacked, again because of you. I wind up with a handful of shit, and my career is now officially over and done. I might as well quit and work as a CPA or something. So excuse the fuck out of me if I wanted my last chance to build a big case and put one in the win column."

I gazed at him in amazement, and actually felt a twinge of sympathy. "I didn't know, sorry. You could have told me all this a while back, you know."

"Yeah, like I'm going to discuss my shitty career path with a known felon."

I laughed. "You just did."

He snorted. "Well, it's not like I've got anything to lose anymore."

"Coffee's ready. You want some?"

"Why not?"

I poured us each a cup and put out a spoon for him. He scooped in four heaps of sugar, and I shook my head in disapproval. He ignored me, stirring the sugar in. I drank deep, savoring the first caffeinated slurp of the morning.

He seemed to have calmed down a notch. "Tell me about this reporter."

He was a federal agent, after all, and much as we didn't like each other, he might come across some information at some point, with resources I didn't have. So I told him.

He chewed his lip. "What's the connection with the church?"

"Don't know yet. The landlady said the reporter had gone there. So I went out last night to see what was up."

"What'd you find out?"

"Squat. But I had a chat with the preacher. Seemed like a nice guy. Is he the one you're after?"

"You know I can't comment."

"I've been square with you. At least tell me what I'm up against. Maybe she was looking into the same thing you were."

He shrugged. "It's a big new church. They got some sizable donations to build it. We want to know where all the money came from. That and a couple of other things."

"So what's the problem?"

"If this woman was kidnapped, that means bringing in the Bureau. And FBI jurisdiction means my case is gone again. Goddammit."

"Maybe you guys should work together some time. Just saying."

"Wouldn't that be nice?"

"They do nice lab work though. Maybe they can lift some prints out of her apartment."

He thought about it. "They'll have to know where the request to dust a place came from."

My coffee was gone, so I poured another cup. I'd probably need it, the way things were going. "Can't you just say it was a tip from a confidential informant?"

"I could, but then I'm on the hook if they don't turn up anything. They don't like doing work that doesn't lead to a bust, and they'd rip my ass to pieces."

I certainly knew their shortcomings, as they'd been the reason I had gone to prison a long time ago. "Just say you heard a tip on a possible abduction. Doesn't have to involve your case. Might not be related."

"They'll want to know every detail, every player involved." He looked at me. "How'd you know her apartment was tossed? They going to find your fingerprints?"

"No, but I did talk to the landlady. Didn't give her my name, though."

"Shit. They may still track you down. If they find out you're involved, that's going to complicate matters."

That was an understatement. This was already getting messy. Murrow had given the landlady his name. If they questioned him, they'd get to me. And when the landlady told them someone had broken in the night before, I'd suddenly need an alibi. If they couldn't track down the fake cops or the prize lady, they'd just focus on me, the guy with a record and a lot to hide. It would divert the whole investigation, and just get me in trouble. Maybe it was best to let it slide for now.

Fielding watched me as I worked this through. "Having second thoughts?"

I remained silent, trying to find a way out that didn't lead to me bearing all the brunt of scrutiny by the FBI. If they were brought in, they'd make me the fall guy. And I'd wind up back in prison.

Dale T. Phillips

CHAPTER 10

My new shrink, Sanders, was wearing a Hawaiian shirt, shorts, and boat shoes with no socks. He looked very comfortable, as if we weren't having a session to discuss my mixed-up and dangerous state of mind. Ah, well, it was a Saturday, and maybe this wasn't during regular office hours. I'd decided to trust him to a certain degree, and be brutally honest about my past and my present. Unusual, since I didn't do this for most people.

"So how have you been since we last spoke, Mr. Taylor?"

I laughed, but it came out a bit on the harsh side. "Let's see. I got involved in finding a missing person, went to church, almost got caught breaking into a place, was chased out by a tiny yapping dog, and had a visit from a

Treasury agent who might get the FBI on my ass and have me thrown back in prison."

He peered at me over his glasses, not rattled in the least. "Impressive. All that in less than forty-eight hours. I see why you say your life is complicated."

I spread my hands. "Told you I was a mess."

"Let's work it through. Missing person?"

"Someone thought I could help. I ask around, see what's up, go digging."

He raised his eyebrows. "So you *do* help people."

"Sometimes. More often I make it worse."

"If someone's missing, that's pretty bad, right? So you can do some good."

I rubbed my hands on my thighs. "If I don't go to jail first."

"The break-in? What was that about?"

"Not stealing anything. Just got into the missing woman's apartment to look for clues. But someone had already searched it."

"And the Treasury and FBI problem?"

"If they investigate the missing woman case, they'll discover my involvement. And then it's all about *me* instead of her."

"Got it. So you went to church. Did it change your mind about anything?"

I shook my head. "Still part of the missing woman puzzle. She went there, so I did, too.

Spoke with a preacher who had some pretty bad problems. He seems to deal with them better than me."

"How?"

"He tries to help people as best he can, and lets God handle it."

"Something to be said for that approach."

I sighed. "Too passive for me. I can't just let everything go and trust it'll come out okay. It's like AA with that higher power stuff."

"Anchors are good. Religion is one. Family's another. Tell me about yours."

My tone was a little sharp. "We stopped being a family when my brother died."

He paused for a moment, and I thought he was going to pull on that lever, but he let it pass. "Friends?"

"I came to Maine to investigate the murder of my best friend. I've stayed since, trying to build something, but it all keeps falling apart."

"And your romantic involvement with the young woman?"

"Allison? Her life went to shit, too, all because of me."

Sanders took off his glasses and polished them with the hem of his island shirt. "Sounds like you're Lucifer incarnate."

His comment surprised me. "Well, it's not like I *try* to fuck up everything."

"No, but you may be trying to sabotage *yourself.* Missing persons case? Usually the police handle something like that."

"You told me to find something else to focus on. And J.C. asked me to get involved."

"So there are intelligent, caring people who trust you and your abilities, despite your colorful history."

"I guess."

"What is it you think they see in you?"

I shrugged. "My rapier-like wit and dashing good looks?"

"We both know that's not it. Humorous defense mechanism aside, what are the qualities in you that good people like?"

"Loyalty, I suppose. And I try to do the right things, though it doesn't always come out that way."

He tapped a pen. "And the people that aren't so nice? How do they view you?"

"As a major pain in the ass."

"Because you won't let them get away with hurting others, correct?"

"You could see it that way."

"So you have a flawed system, but it works, after a fashion. You realize, don't you, that's how most people get through life?"

I picked at the arm of the chair. "Most people's systems don't have the body count that mine has."

"Most people aren't taking on the kind of things and people you do. Oh, I've read the newspaper stories, and J.C. has filled me in on some other details. That feeling you get like you're ready to explode? That comes from bottling things up inside."

"Who can I talk to? With the box of demons I have, most people would run screaming. Allison got a glimpse, and look what it did to her."

He shrugged. "I've heard worse. Those veterans I told you about. A lot of people with tragic life stories that would peel the paint off a house, the horror is so blistering. They don't have a mission, and they don't try to be a knight-errant. They just wonder how they can go on with what they've seen."

"And how do they?"

"With a lot of help, and one day at a time. I told you, you have to find something external, some purpose. Your lady friend is going to have to as well. The world she knew is gone. She's going to have to move on to something else."

"I'm worried that something else might not include me."

"That may be. You fell in love, and it's not going well. Sometimes two people cannot be together, no matter how much they love each other."

I sat up and gave him a stare. "I didn't come here to hear that."

"Well, I could blow smoke up your ass, tell you everything is going to be okay, but you wouldn't believe me anyway. This way, at least I keep a little credibility, even if you hate what I'm saying."

I was quiet, my emotions boiling inside me. "What do I do now?"

"J.C. put you on a mission. He said that makes you focus. It's a good cause, so stick with that."

"What if I'm just a ticking time bomb?"

He leaned forward. "I've had people in that chair that were told they had cancer, and not long to live. Some just fold up and stop living right there, and some go out and live as much as they can in the time they have left. Which type are you?"

I thought it over. "I guess I'm not ready to pack it in just yet."

"Well that's a start now, isn't it?"

CHAPTER 11

The matchbook from Georgette's apartment was from a place called Jimmy's Joint, a strip club out on Congress Street. Interesting that my leads took me from a church to a stage where women took off their clothes and danced for money. I guess Georgette was covering all the bases.

Strip clubs aren't that much excitement for me. Seeing it took me back to a time when I'd been a bodyguard to men with money. In the course of that employment I'd seen too many strip joints, accompanying a class of males who needed to act the big spender at clubs like this, throwing cash at the dancers and pouring champagne, to let everyone know who was the big dog. They loved the way the dancers would shower them with attention, but all the women wanted was to pull more bills out of their wallet.

A good bodyguard watches the crowd, not the women dancing. If you want to know about the male of the species, spend some time at a strip club. Study the unsmiling ones who stare at a woman's body like a hungry wolf eyes a wounded elk it wants to rip into. They're the scary ones, and you fear what they'll do after they leave, like a loaded gun, to go through the general populace, among wives, and daughters, and mothers. Most of the rest just act like jerks, either trying too hard to be cool, or behaving like horny teenagers, nudging each other and cracking crude sexual jokes. It'll make you wonder why women have anything to do with men.

As a bodyguard in a place like this, there are times when your employer is getting some additional personal services, like a private lap dance or something even more physical, and you just sit around waiting for him to finish. Occasionally one of the dancers will be so bored she'll actually talk to you, even though it's obvious you're not a mark to make money from. Sometimes they'll be surprisingly open about their lives and how they feel about their job. A lot of them despise the leering, pawing louts who see them only as sex objects. Others don't mind the work, and some really enjoy it. They love the control they have, teasing and stoking the unchecked lust, making a game of getting the most money out of the marks, like carnival hucksters.

Some people view club dancers as all the same, barely one step removed from hookers, but there's a surprising variance. Sure, there are a fair number of party girls who like the easy money and available drugs, but some are students, working to pay for an overpriced degree, and some are single moms with kids to feed, struggling with the bills after the dad took off and left them with nothing. I'd even had good conversations about books with some of them from time to time.

But I never dated any of them. In those days, I kept my emotions locked down, which made for a much easier life. I was a good bodyguard because I just didn't care about anything but the job, and I didn't get distracted. You mix business with pleasure, you get in trouble fast. Part of the rest was fearing to let loose my feelings, and part was acting the macho man like the hard-ass wiseguys whose circles I moved in.

Jimmy's Joint had a doorman, like all of these places, who charged me a few bucks to get in. I let my eyes adjust from the brightness outside to the dimness within. Since it was an afternoon, there was only one stage in play, with a pole in the center. Two guys were along the rail of the stage, two more sat at a table, and one was by himself at the bar.

The silicone-enhanced woman on the stage swayed to the music, something from an eighties hair band that I hadn't heard in years, and hadn't missed. She dipped and humped and tried snakelike movements, eyeing the two seated at the stage. One with a baseball cap on backwards placed a bill on the rail, and she bent over backwards to get it, winking at the guy, who nudged his partner.

I took a seat at a table, and soon a young blonde woman came by in heels, a T-shirt and a miniskirt to ask me what I'd like to drink. She had words tattooed on her arm, but I couldn't read them. She was wearing a lot of makeup, and didn't look me in the eye. I ordered a soda water and lime, and she listlessly moved away.

The woman on stage seemed to be trying to coax more cash from the first guy, playfully tugging her G-string down, first one side, then the other. It worked, and the guy parted with another bill. Free enterprise at its finest.

The young lady returned with my drink, for which I paid a few more dollars. I showed her the picture of Georgette. "Do you know if this woman was in here?"

"You a cop?"

"No. You must be new if you think I'm a cop."

She left and I saw her go straight to the doorman for a quick chat. *Shit.*

He was over by my table a minute later. "Sir? Are you with the police? "

"No. I don't know what she told you, but—"

"That doesn't matter. This is on you. I'm going to have to ask you to leave."

"I just wanted to see if anyone had seen this woman." I flashed the picture of Georgette, but it didn't distract him, and he kept his gaze on me. He knew what he was doing.

"The management has strict rules against asking the ladies questions like that. We don't want any trouble."

"Can I speak to whoever's in charge? I'll explain—"

"The management is not in right now. Please, sir. You have to go."

I stood up. He was built right for a doorman. I could take him, but he was just doing his job, and it wouldn't get me anything. He hadn't copped any attitude. I nodded. "Been in your shoes before. No trouble."

"I appreciate that, sir. Sorry."

"Any idea when the boss will be around?"

"Afraid I couldn't say, sir."

Of course not. Feeling a deep sense of frustration, I left. But I'd be back.

CHAPTER 12

J.C. asked me to dine with him at one of his nice hangouts, a place that was all dark wood, tasteful brass, and quiet corners for patrons to enjoy a bit of privacy. It was early for a Saturday, so we had the place mostly to ourselves. He sipped his Scotch, and I had my usual former-drinker favorite, soda water and lime.

I was hoping for some good news. "Heard anything about Allison?"

"Just that she's painting up a storm, and seems to have fewer nightmares."

"That's good. Any word on when we can see her?"

"Not yet. But it sounds like they're helping her. I know it's rough."

"That's an understatement."

"Is that why you're breaking into places?" He swirled his glass. "Oh, don't screw your face up like that."

"Bob told you, huh?"

"He's worried about you. He doesn't want you to go to jail because of what he asked you to do."

"I had to get in there some way. But the place had been searched already. A couple of guys posed as cops earlier, tried to get in. The landlady wouldn't let them. Next thing, she miraculously wins a contest she didn't even enter, and is away for a few hours. My guess is that's when they did it. So there's at least three other people involved, and they wanted to either clean up their trail, or were looking for something."

J.C. frowned. "That's bad, right?"

"No, that's great. With that many involved, it means there's something for me to go on. She wasn't grabbed by some random nut job who it would be impossible to trace."

"Did you find anything?"

"Only a matchbook from a strip club called Jimmy's Joint. I went down there to ask questions, but the doorman threw me out."

J.C. laughed.

"What's so funny?"

"It was Nick, right?" J.C. described the doorman.

"That's the guy. You know him?"

"You should have asked me to go with you."

I stared at him. "You don't seem like the type."

"Jimmy Saperstein owns the place. His people and I go way back. In fact, it's a family business. His father tends bar, his brother is the deejay, Nick's a cousin, and Jimmy's mom even sews costumes for the girls."

"I didn't see many costumes in my brief visit."

"Why waste them on the afternoon crowd?"

I shook my head in disbelief. "So you can get me permission from the bossman to ask questions?"

"We'll go after dinner."

I twirled my pasta on a fork. "Can I ask you something without you getting offended?"

"Doubtful. You'll just have to risk my wrath."

"Think there might be something of a non-legal nature at Jimmy's that would interest Georgette?"

He paused, considering the question. "Nothing heavy, not as part of the club. It's not like other places, the ones run by the mob in particular. The Sapersteins aren't connected to any mobsters, and they've owned the place for years. They don't allow drugs in the club. Anybody caught gets chucked out. Maybe some of the girls turn tricks on the side, but they better not get caught at that, either. If they were running anything bad, think your buddy Lieutenant McClaren would let them stay open?"

"He's not my buddy. But point taken. I'm just wondering why Georgette would have gone there after a story."

J.C. raised his eyebrows. "You ever consider maybe her interest might have been personal, rather than professional?"

I shrugged. "Murrow said she'd had a couple of boyfriends, though nothing long-term. Who knows? You know a dancer named Carol?"

He shook his head. "Doesn't ring a bell. Why?"

"Her name was scribbled on the matchbook. I know it's a slim lead, but it's all I've got, apart from the church."

We were early for a Saturday night at the strip club, but it was more populated than it had been hours before. Nick the doorman greeted J.C. warmly. Then he saw me, and his face darkened.

J.C. smiled at him and nodded toward me. "I'm taking him to see Jimmy."

Nick nodded back and let me pass. It never failed to amaze me who J.C. knew, and what connections he had, even in the most unlikely places. The magic pass of familiarity, and J.C. seemed to have the key to the city. He stopped to greet the deejay and the bartender, and even a few of the dancers and cocktail waitresses. He took me past the bar to a door, and the bartender buzzed us through to a set of stairs that led up. We got to the top, and looked through an open office door.

"Jimmy," J.C. called out, and was met by a tall, sharp-faced guy who embraced him like a brother. They chatted for a minute, and J.C. introduced me.

"Jimmy, this is Zack. I brought him by because he found one of your matchbooks in the place of a young woman who's missing. A reporter. He wants to know if any of your people have seen her."

"Ah, you're the one," said Jimmy, offering his hand. "Nick told me you'd been by."

I shook. "Your man was very professional."

"Thanks for not causing trouble. Lotta people looking for an angle, and we get a fair number of whack jobs. Nick keeps it tight down there. We don't want any fuss."

"I don't want to disrupt things. A woman asking questions in a club tends to get noticed. So maybe somebody remembers."

"Okay, let me come down and clear it so you can ask around. If J.C. says you're okay, then you've got special privileges."

"Much obliged."

Downstairs, Jimmy went over to talk to Nick at the door. When they were done, Jimmy went behind the bar, while Nick walked away and came back a minute later with another guy who took a seat at the door. Nick then came over to us.

"We're cool," he said, extending his hand. I shook to show there were no hard feelings.

"No worries. Like I said, been there too."

"How do you want to do this?"

"It's busy, and I don't want to get in the way. If you want to start with the waitresses, bring each one over when they have a sec. Shouldn't take long at all."

Nick went away to find my first interview.

J.C. said he was going to get a drink. "How much money do you have on you?"

"Couple hundred. Why?"

"I'm going to let you do this by yourself, which I know you prefer. And they're likely to tell you more if you're by yourself. Give every woman a twenty for her time."

"I know how this works, remember."

"Just making sure."

J.C. left and Nick came up with a waitress in tow. "Wendy, this is Zack. He's not a cop, but he's going to ask some questions. Answer him truthfully, no bullshit. Anything good gets you a gold star."

I showed the picture. "Do you know if she was in here? A week or more ago?"

She shook her head in the negative. I thanked her and handed her a twenty. Hell of a price for being a good guy.

On it went as the music pulsed in song after song, first the waitresses, then the dancers, whenever one had a break. Now I saw the costumes, as if it was Halloween: nurses, cowgirls, dominatrixes, a cheerleader, all designed to entice various male fantasies, but all with platform heels. After the first couple of women, my nose twitched from the mix of perfumes like at a large department store makeup counter. Most of the dancers had long hair, and almost all had visible tattoos. A couple of them thought the woman in the picture looked familiar. Had it been a man, I doubt they'd have recognized him. After I'd spoken to half a dozen women, I finally got a hit.

She took the picture in her hand and flicked a polished nail against it. "Yeah, she was here. Wanted to ask questions, like you."

"Nick didn't ask her to leave?"

She gave me a look that said I was an idiot. "She's not a *guy*. That's a different story entirely. She talked for a few minutes, but it looked like she was fishing. Asking about drugs, hooking, that kind of thing. Everybody knows Jimmy doesn't put up with that shit. She asked a few of the girls, but I don't think she got the angle she was looking for. Didn't see her after that."

"You know someone here named Carol?"

The woman frowned. "That one. We get special guest appearances from out-of-town talent, and she was here last week. Someone saw her taking a toot, though, and Jimmy bounced her ass out."

"Any idea how I can get in touch with her?"

"Ask Jimmy."

I gave her a pair of twenties and spoke with the rest of the women. Two other dancers recognized Georgette, and the story was the same. Yes, she'd been in one time, asked a few questions, and left.

When I'd gone through all the women, I went back for a chat with Jimmy.

"Can you tell me about this Carol?"

He shook his head and looked like he wanted to spit. "Why I don't like out-of-town talent. Everybody here knows the rules, but you get someone in who thinks they can do whatever they want, soon the trouble starts."

"Then why do it at all?"

"Money, what else? Our clientele loves it, gets us more coming in when there's a special guest star. Some of them are adult film actresses, that kind of thing. Guys want their picture taken with them, and then spend like sailors on leave."

"How do you find this talent?"

"An agency."

"So what happened with this one?"

"She was supposed to be here all week, but we don't want cokeheads. Two different people caught her, so I told her to hit the bricks, her contract was canceled."

"How'd she take it?"

"About like you'd expect. Screamed she was gonna sue me until I told her I'd call the cops. Then she told me how she knew these guys who would come and burn down my club and kill my family. That's when I brought out the tape recorder and played her threat back to her. That shut her up. I reported her to the agency, too."

"You're not worried?"

"Every one of them who comes through here and messes up will tell us what she can have done to us. We've been here for fourteen years, and I carry a gun. So no, I'm not worried."

"I see. Still, she may have contacted the woman I'm looking for. Do you mind if I talk to her?"

"No skin off my nose. She won't be coming back to Maine."

"How would I get in touch with her? That agency?"

"If they haven't canned her by now. Let me make a couple calls."

Jimmy was on the phone for a few minutes and handed me a piece of paper with an address on it.

"She's at a club in Worcester, down in Mass. That's the hotel she's staying at. Good luck."

I thanked him and went to collect J.C.

Georgette had not left much of a trail, just a ghostly whisper. I hoped it would be enough. And I worried over the fact that she'd disappeared after asking inconvenient questions at a strip club.

CHAPTER 13

The night after the strip club found me back in church, somewhere I hadn't been on a Sunday morn since I was an early teen. I recognized a number of faces from the Friday night service. There were quite a few new ones, too, as the crowd swelled to about double what it had been the night before last. The air had an almost festive mood, people whispering to their neighbors, seeming to anticipate a real event.

Someone roaming the aisle locked his gaze on me, a hard-case guy in a dark suit with a tell-tale bulge underneath one arm that said he was packing. In that crowd he stood out like a wolf among sheep. He was by himself and had been closely scanning the faces in the crowd. I instantly pegged him as security, and gave him a goofy, dim smile to show I wasn't a threat. For once I wanted to lay low and scout out the territory first.

His face was pitted, and his sparse hair was slicked back. His gaze lingered on me a long moment before moving on. I looked around and noticed two other standout suits at various locales, and thought it was pretty heavy security for a church service. Another guy came up to speak with Hard-case, a thin man about my height, with overly coiffed hair, thick, black glasses like Buddy Holly's, and an expensive suit that stood out among the more mundane garb around us. He was certainly no muscle. The two of them looked around and conferred some more, and Buddy Holly walked down the aisle toward the back.

The reason for all the buzz became apparent as a woman walked in with Buddy, and the noise level increased. Since her image was splashed everywhere around Portland, and probably all of Maine, I recognized her as Helen Schiller, who was running for Senator. All eyes were on her as she strolled in, waving and smiling as if this was a campaign stop. Maybe it was. She shook many hands on her way up the aisle, and the people seemed smitten with her judging from the rapt look on their faces.

Buddy Holly shadowed her as she took a seat down front and sat beside her. Hard-case sat on the other side. The other two security hounds I'd spotted stayed standing in the back. The buzz died down a little as the preacher came out.

"I see we have a distinguished visitor today. Everybody, please welcome our next Senator from the great state of Maine, Helen Schiller." He finished to thunderous applause. I didn't join in, not liking the mixing of church and state. If churches were going to get a free ride on taxes, they should stay the hell out of politics.

After that it got down to the usual business of churching. It seemed to me that the preacher was getting a good boost from the crowd, and his sermon had some pizzazz to it. But none of it affected me so I wondered why I'd returned. I told myself if Georgette had come here looking for a story, it was likely the financial angle. But then that nagging little voice in my head said that there was more to it. Or maybe she'd turned up something dark at the strip club.

My mind wandered, picking up impressions. Nothing rang any bells until it came time for the collection. A nervous kid I'd seen before was one of those passing out the baskets. I studied his face, and saw he bore a physical resemblance to the preacher. Ah. His son that he'd talked about, the one that had problems. What kind of problems? Worth checking into.

When the service ended, there were some announcements. Among them was the news that the distinguished Ms. Schiller would be attending a 4-H festival up the road after church. Everyone stood, and a small crowd gathered around the politician. Her security man and Buddy Holly cleared a way for her, as she told everyone they could all talk outside. Now that I wasn't being watched, I scrutinized her guard dog. I didn't like what I saw. As a former bouncer and security man, I had trained myself to spot the bad characters, and this guy had all the signs of a dangerous predator. He watched other people with shark's eyes, black and pitiless, and I had no doubt he'd shoot anyone who gave him an excuse. Guys like this stick out because you don't see them every day. And not often in church. There's professional security men, and then there's another level. Was Senator-to-be that dangerous a role in Maine?

Schiller had moved to an open area where her throng of admirers had space to gather around, and a few took pictures. The preacher was there with her, and they were all chatting up a storm. I looked around and saw the jittery kid hanging out at the edge of the crowd, now looking bored as hell. I sidled up next to him.

"Hey, how's it going?"

He startled like a spooked horse, and looked around like I'd accused him of something.

I nodded toward the preacher. "You're his son, right?"

"Uh, yeah."

Before we got any further in the conversation, the security guy suddenly appeared before me. He spoke to the kid from the side of his mouth. "Bobby, your father wants to talk to you."

The kid shot me one nervous look before he bolted away. Mr. Security was now right in my personal space, close enough for me to smell his aftershave, some sort of Bay Rum. He used too much of it. His black eyes bored into me, as if he was trying to read my thoughts.

"Can I help you?" I put on the pleasant smile, forcing myself to dial my reactions back a little.

"You were asking about someone being here. A woman." And to top it off, his breath reeked of stale onion, or something equally as bad.

I pulled forth the photo of Georgette. "Yes, this woman. Have you seen her?"

"No." His gaze hadn't left my face.

My smile disappeared, and my voice got a bit sharp. "You might try actually looking at the picture first."

"Who are you and what do you want?"

I held up a finger. "You need to learn some manners." I was getting in a mood to give him a lesson. It would get ugly fast if he didn't back down.

"You boys play nice, now." The voice came from my right. I took my gaze off Mr. Security and saw Buddy Holly swooping in to keep us from starting anything. He pushed up his glasses and grinned a broad, toothy welcome, like he was a used-car salesman with a great deal for us.

"Look at you two, ready to butt heads like a couple of bighorn sheep. I'm Daniel Colby, assistant to Ms. Schiller," he said, stepping in. "I'm afraid Lester here is a bit overprotective when it comes to the Senator." He smiled at us. "But he means well. Lester, Ms. Schiller could use your help."

Hard-case gave Colby a look intended to be menacing, then gave me one final glare before stalking off.

Colby stuck out a hand. "I don't believe I've had the pleasure, sir."

"Zack Taylor," I said, ignoring the proffered welcome. I wasn't much for shaking with people who hadn't earned it yet.

He ignored it and moved on. "What brings you out to our little church service in the woods?"

"This young woman," I showed him the picture. "Have you seen her?"

He pushed up his glasses again, studied the photo, and nodded. "Yes, I believe so, but she wasn't a regular here. I hadn't actually met her. Is she a friend of yours?"

"Friend of a friend."

"Is she in some sort of trouble?"

"I don't know," I said. "She seems to have gone missing, and people are worried about her."

"Well, if our office can be of any help, let me know." He slipped me a business card. "How about if you send us this photo, and I'll have the staff keep an eye out. And we'll check if anybody has seen her."

"That would be nice," I said.

"Okay, then," he smiled again. "Nice meeting you, Zack Taylor. I'll get back to making myself useful. We'll see you around."

It sounded friendly, but I felt a chill, and couldn't explain why.

Dale T. Phillips

CHAPTER 14

When Schiller's entourage left the church in two vehicles, I followed. She was in the back of a Lincoln Continental driven by Colby, with the head security guy in the passenger seat. The other two got to tag along in a black SUV.

They drove about fifteen miles up the road to a fairgrounds, and got flagged through the main gate for parking. I went to the lot across the road with everyone else, where teenagers wearing orange vests waved flags to direct me where to put my car. I followed the crowd back across the road and paid my few bucks to get into the 4-H county fair.

The smell of fried dough, popcorn, and farm animals took me back. I heard the baaing of sheep, and a cow responded with a low, mournful call. People were cheery and smiling, families walking together to view the displays, either open or in booths, and of course there were the food stands. I strolled through the indoor arena, glancing at the displays of prize-winning vegetables. I'd never won a blue ribbon, or any color for that matter, for my string beans or anything from a garden. But my family had raised turkeys and this fair brought back the time of hauling the birds to competitions to be judged. It had been a real pain in the ass. The family business link stirred up memories of my dead brother, so I shut down thoughts of the past. I had too many ghosts haunting me and didn't need another one right now to distract me. It made me a little sad to think that I was one of the few people so emotionally crippled that I couldn't even have a good time at this wholesome display of Americana.

I found Schiller's group, surrounded by a knot of people. Not wanting to be confronted by the security guy again, I eased into the crowd and made myself inconspicuous. Schiller was talking, Colby was passing out fliers, and the security guy was conversing with a man in farm clothes holding a walkie-talkie.

Helen Schiller was about five-foot-four, trim, late forties, with a thin face and intense gaze. She was smiling the politician smile but it stopped at her mouth, and her eyes were cold. I noticed a small scar above her eyebrow, not as bad as mine. It made her look serious but was probably an asset in her line of work.

When Schiller paused in her pitch, I saw my chance and pushed my way to the front, rudely nudging aside a woman who had opened her mouth to speak.

"Ms. Schiller, could I talk to you for just a minute?"

She turned her gaze on me. She had dirty-blonde hair and weathered skin. Her chin was pointed and foxlike, and she gave a direct, hard stare from dark eyes. Her eyebrows knit together in a microsecond of scowl before her face relaxed into the professional politician smile.

"Certainly. What can I do for you?"

"Have you seen this woman out at the Church of the Redeemer?" I held up the photo of Georgette. There was a flash of recognition across her features, and something else that I couldn't place. It was gone so quickly that if I hadn't been watching closely, I'd have missed it. The smile was now forced.

"Why don't you speak with Daniel, my assistant?"

"Are you saying you haven't seen her?"

She narrowed her eyes. "Don't be rude, young man. Daniel, can you help this gentleman?"

She turned away and someone else spoke to her. Everyone around me was giving me the stink eye like I'd laughed at a funeral.

Colby took my elbow. "Why don't you step this way?"

I saw the security guy with a red face, his mouth a tight slash, and boring holes into me with his stare. I shrugged and walked away with Colby.

He also didn't look happy. "I told you, send me the picture, and we'll ask around. Please don't bother the Senator like that."

"Like what? It was a simple question."

"Are you trying to cause some sort of trouble? Who do you work for?"

I laughed. "What, you think this is political?"

He shrugged. "We never know what they'll try. Okay, so you're not for the other team. But if you're attempting to be annoying, you're succeeding. We have enough issues to deal with, and we get a lot of people trying to bother the candidate. We don't prefer to have them do it with things that really aren't our problem."

"So I won't be getting an invite to the inauguration?"

Colby sighed and gave me a look. He motioned to the other two security guys just a few feet away, waiting for his signal. "Boys, would you show Mr. Taylor around? Be nice, but make sure he stays away from the Senator."

"She's not Senator yet, is she?"

Colby plastered on a smile that he in no way felt. "Enjoy the fair, Mr. Taylor."

Dale T. Phillips

CHAPTER 15

Murrow looked like hell: rumpled, unshaven, and bleary-eyed, like he hadn't slept for a couple of days, and had been worried the whole time. I met him on the sunny trail around Back Cove used by all the fitness buffs and nature lovers. We were sitting on a bench while he was chain smoking, garnering evil looks from the healthy-minded folk who passed by.

"Have you found out anything?" He seemed desperate for any piece of good news that might indicate his young reporter was alive and well.

"I believe you."

Those few words seemed to remove a huge weight from his shoulders. He put his head in his hands, and looked about to break down. Once again I was reminded of the cost of caring for someone and feeling responsible. I wasn't a toucher but he needed some support, so I put a hand on his shoulder.

"There's definitely something going on," I said, and filled him in. "The good news is, with that many people involved, it's not some random lone guy, which would be worse news. More people means more threads for me to pull on, and a chance to find something."

He looked at me with desperate hope in his eyes. "How can I help?"

"What can you tell me about Helen Schiller?"

He frowned. "What's she got to do with it?"

I shrugged. "Maybe nothing. But the people around her are off. She seems like a big wheel at the church, and Georgette went to the church. So I started there and asked around."

He paused and stubbed out his cigarette. He took out another and lit up. Seeing my face, he looked sheepish. "Filthy habit, I know. I started up again when she disappeared."

"Stress will do that."

He let out some smoke and looked pensive. "How to describe our next Senator-to-be…"

I looked out over the water as I waited for him to gather his thoughts.

"She's what you get when you cross the uneducated and prejudiced side of the backwoods with a ruthless desire to make others follow your narrow path. At some point she found she could get a platform for all her views, get revenge on the people who crossed her, and get paid for working her agenda. Rabidly anti-government and anti-tax, as if bridges, roads, and schools build themselves. Hugely pro-gun, no restrictions. We had a big story where a hunter shot a mother of two in her own back yard, then left her there to bleed to death. Schiller said it was the woman's fault, because she was wearing brown mittens during hunting season. Sounds crazy, but it really happened. Schiller is against using public money to build anything new, even hospitals. Oh, and she was violently against the casinos they always want to put up. Her speeches were screeds *against* so many things, you couldn't tell what she was *for*. Then that all changed."

"What happened?"

He paused for effect. "She killed a man. Shot him down on her front porch. A political rival."

"Holy cow. And she got away with it?"

"Claimed self-defense. Hell, if a hunter up here can gun down a mother in her own back yard and walk free, killing someone on your porch doesn't mean squat. There were no other witnesses. I read that he was found with a gun, sold at one of the many gun shows around the state without paperwork. So she claimed self-defense, and it was open and shut."

Murrow stopped for a long drag. "While she got away with it, it did put the kibosh on her career ambitions. She was never really popular with anyone except the worst of the Second Amendment crowd. Rubbed people the wrong way, stepped on a lot of toes, and didn't seem to care who she pissed off. Went after a bunch of people who got in her path, one way or another. After she killed the guy, the political parties didn't want to have anything to do with her. So the support dried up, and more importantly, the funding. She got slaughtered in a run for governor and looked to be headed for the scrap heap. Then a miracle happened."

Murrow took out another cigarette and looked at it for a moment but didn't light it. "She comes out with a new coat of polish, new positions, and a smooth-talking, constant companion by the name of Daniel Colby, who, it's whispered, formerly worked for a casino syndicate. With him as the power behind the throne, her speeches transformed into things a real politician would say. She could now work with people, compromise and cooperate. There's a big religious radio station that suddenly was pushing her as the Great White Hope, having her on for interviews, playing her speeches, promoting the hell out of her. And money. She went from nothing to having what seems like an unlimited war chest for campaigning. Which is coincidental, because she turned *very* pro-casino. Their attempts had been headed for the scrap heap as well, but a new state bill to allow more of them is now a major part of her agenda."

He paused again. "And she got more vocal about some other things."

I prompted him. "Such as?"

"She'd always had a streak of racism but now it's got shiny packaging, thinly disguised as concern for the unemployed, among other things. She got good at conning people that someone else is responsible for their being downtrodden and out of work. Like the Somalis."

"Somalis?"

"Yeah, there's a big influx into the Lewiston area. If there are problems involving anyone from that community, you bet she's quick to jump on it and make it seem like a crime epidemic. There are rumors she acquired backers who are even scarier than casino hoods. Certain organizations where the members have shaved heads and German WWII-type tattoos."

"White supremacists."

"There are some pockets around the state. And they sure as hell don't support the Somalis moving in."

"Hell of a constituency."

"Yeah. Supposedly, her security man Lester was one of their enforcers out west, got into some trouble and was transferred here. So with all that money and backing, and telling an audience whatever they want to hear, she's gaining in popularity. She finally got some party backers on her side. There's a good chance she'll win, and that'll be bad for the people of Maine, you can bet on it. You should listen to some of her speeches on that station. It'll show you what I'm talking about."

"Think maybe that's the kind of stuff Georgette was checking into?"

He paused. "If she found a link she'd have been all over that."

"So maybe she asked the right questions of the wrong people. I'll go kicking some hornets' nests, see what I can find."

"People aren't going to be too happy with you. I don't want you getting hurt because I put you onto this."

"I'll be careful," I lied. "So what's the connection with the Church of the Redeemer and the radio station?"

"More of Schiller's new buddies. Caleb Martin was also a casino opponent, and had to work through his own scandal. He had a former church, a tiny one. Got one of his young parishioners pregnant. It was hushed up, but word leaked out. His wife died soon after. Some say it wasn't an accident, that she killed herself. So he got serious, did the sackcloth and ashes thing for a long time, and is now a repentant sinner. But with a big, new church. The station did major fundraising for it, and has him on as a guest speaker all the time. But there was a lot more money from somewhere else. Like for the pregnant girl's family who lived in a trailer in the woods, but one day left town and moved to the coast, into a big spread."

"Bought off?"

He waved his still unlit cigarette. "Sure looks like it."

"Do you know where they are now?"

"I can find out."

"Do that. And see if you can get me any info on the casino people behind Schiller. I'd love to chat with some of them."

"I don't think they're likely to tell you anything."

"Maybe not. But I'd like to see if they get nervous when I start hanging around and asking questions. Then I see what their next move is."

Murrow coughed. "You know, someone else was writing about Schiller. Guy named Mason Carter."

I frowned.

He nodded. "You know about him, huh?"

"Yeah. Are you seriously telling me I have to talk to that creep?"

"Well, he was writing about her. When she shot the guy, he coined the term 'Killer Schiller.' Was doing a whole series, and then he just stopped."

"Be interesting to find out why, and what else he might have turned up."

"Which means you'll have to talk to him."

I sighed. "Afraid so."

"Punch him one for me," Murrow said, and gave a mirthless laugh. "Can't stand the little weasel."

CHAPTER 16

The scandal sheet that Mason Carter worked for had a tip line, so I called them with a fake story about a hot item if they could tell me where Carter was. I found him covering an outdoor festival in Deering Oaks Park. He was speaking to someone in a chicken costume. Ah, the glamorous life of the intrepid journalist. I actually felt a little sorry for him.

Nevertheless, I snuck up behind Carter to surprise him. "Why did the chicken cross the road?"

He gave a startled squawk and spun around. "You."

"Yup."

Whoever was in the chicken suit laughed. "Haw. Oughta see your face, Carter. Looks like you don't know whether to shit or go blind."

"Shut up," said Carter to the chicken. He made a face at me. "What do you want? You still owe me for that camera."

"You stuck that camera where it didn't belong. Be glad that's the only thing that got broken."

"You threatening me? Again? In front of a witness?"

"Nah, water under the bridge. I heard you did some stories on someone I just met."

His grin spread wide, but it made him look like a Batman villain. "So now you want my help? What's in it for me?"

"What can you tell me about Helen Schiller?"

The grin vanished as his mouth went slack and his eyes widened. The blood left his face, and he took a step back.

"Not a goddamned thing."

I cocked my head. "What's the matter? What are you afraid of?"

"I don't have to talk to you, and I'm not going to. Now fuck off."

"Listen, you pushed that 'Shooting Gallery' crap, and slung mud at me again so you could sell papers. You owe me. What the hell's so scary about Killer Schiller?"

He turned and ran. Just ran away. I was so surprised, I let him go. I looked at the guy in the chicken suit, who gave an elaborate feathered shrug.

"Don't know what all that was about, but I gotta go sing," he said, and walked over to a stage, flapping his wings as he took a microphone from a stand. His voice boosted by an amplifier, the chicken man started clucking out a song. I didn't stay to listen.

With Carter on the run, my next step was to try to talk to someone else who also probably wouldn't like it, the family of the teenage girl. Murrow had given me the address, and it wasn't far up the coast.

On the way up, I tuned in to the religious station Murrow had told me about. There was a lot of hellfire and brimstone, and talking about the path of sin and the wages of sin. The wages made it sound like a regular job, when I knew it was piecemeal contract work. They used a lot of coded text in their exhortations, but if you knew the lingo, you could tell it was a station for smug white people to be secure in their position at the top of the food chain. Everybody else was going to Hell, and the descriptions of the eternal sufferings of the Damned was in graphic detail. So much for the loving words of Christ. This was strictly Old Testament stuff, without a hint of the empathy of Jesus. It sounded like there was a lot more hate than love in these people.

They mentioned the Church of the Redeemer, and Schiller, numerous times. They even had listings of her appearances for the week, and promises to broadcast a recent speech of hers on Monday. Of course they asked for money, with strong hints that it just might keep the donor on the proper path and pave the way for their salvation. And there was a lot of talk of Armageddon as a sure thing in the near future. These people seemed to relish the end of the world, so they could go to their richly-deserved reward, and to Hell with everybody else. I turned it off, wondering how these people got wired for so much hate for the rest of the human race.

I found the address I was looking for and thought about the value of coastal real estate. For someone from the backwoods, this wasn't just a step up, but a complete plunge into a different lifestyle. The large house by the water had to be worth at least in the neighborhood of a million and a half. One hell of a buyoff.

A woman answered the door, and I put on my Sunday smile. "Mrs. Sirois?"

"What do you want?"

"I'm not selling anything." She relaxed half a tick. "I wonder if you'd talk to me about what happened at the church you used to belong to."

I was ready for a door slam in my face, annoyance, yelling, any of that, but I wasn't prepared for the look of absolute panic and fear.

"Who are you? Go away and leave us alone."

"I thought you might want to talk to someone after all this time."

"We didn't talk. You can tell them, we didn't talk to anyone. And we never will. We've kept our part of the bargain. Now go away before I call the police."

And the door slammed.

I stood there, pondering her words. She was afraid, but of who or what?

As I thought about it, the door opened again, and a portly guy wearing a T-shirt and jeans and a ball cap glowered at me. He charged, enveloping me in his arms and driving me off the steps. I twisted just in time to keep from getting crushed when we fell to earth, and instead it was me on top. The air whoofed out of him, and I rolled off and stood up. I felt a rush of air from behind me, and turned to see an older guy swinging at me with a baseball bat. I pulled back as the swing made a murderous arc, just missing me. He cocked back for another go, but I stepped in, grabbed the bat, and gave him a sharp elbow to the face. As his head rocked back, I pulled on the bat and yanked it away from him. He stretched his arms out to grab me, and I gave him a poke in the belly with the end of the bat. His mouth opened wide, and he took two steps back and sat down on the manicured lawn, holding his stomach.

I extended the bat at the first guy, who was on his hands and knees. "You. What the hell is this about?"

"Fuck off."

"Wrong answer," I said. I stepped behind him and gave him a hard smack on the ass with the bat. He squawked and fell flat on his face. I put a knee in his back, knocked off his cap, and grabbed a handful of greasy hair, pulling his head back. It was stupid and risky to be rolling around on the front lawn of a rich neighborhood like this, but they'd just attacked me, and I had no patience.

"One more time. What's this about?"

"We did what you said. We just want you to leave us alone."

Did they think I was with the people who had set them up here? I decided to play it like I was. "And what did we tell you to do?"

"Keep our mouth shut."

I looked over at the second guy, but he didn't seem eager to get up any time soon. "And in return, you got this nice house and some money."

"Not enough. It's gone already. Know what it costs to live in this neighborhood? Know what the taxes are like?"

"My heart bleeds. Why do you think I'm here?"

"To warn us again. Well, we've been warned enough. We're tired of it."

"And so you decided to fight back."

"We're not afraid of you."

"The woman inside sure was."

He tried to twist around to get up, but my weight on his back and the leverage I had prevented it.

He settled for breathing hard. "You leave her out of this."

"We had a deal, and now it sounds like you're not happy with it."

"You people fucked with our family, made us leave. We don't belong here, never did. But we never talked."

I had a flash of insight. "Not even to the young woman reporter?"

"We didn't tell her shit."

"When did you talk to her?"

"Why you asking? We called you after she left, like we agreed."

"Maybe I didn't get that particular message. What number did you use?"

"The one you people gave us. You said if anyone came snooping around, to call you, let you know."

"Tell me again."

"She showed up here a week ago. We told her to get lost."

"What did she say?"

He was silent, so I yanked a little on his hair.

"She said she knew we were paid to leave town and say nothing, but if we wanted to talk to her, we could finally tell our story. She wanted to know who approached us with the offer."

"Don't talk to him, Reg," the other man wheezed, having finally caught his breath back.

"Fuck it, he already knows this part," the guy under me said. "Probably why he's here."

"That's right," I said. "You're not getting any more money, and you're never getting off the hook. People will keep asking, and you can't use a bat on all of them." I was showboating, hoping to make them see that it did them no good to remain silent. "Now I'm going to let you up, and you're going to go inside and get me that number, so we can make sure you got the right one. I'll keep your buddy company. If you try anything, shit's going to get bad for all of you."

I had no idea what I was doing, but if I had a phone number, I had another lead.

Dale T. Phillips

CHAPTER 17

Despite a public disturbance that could have landed me back in jail, I was feeling no closer to finding Georgette, and I still didn't know where to look. My mood was blacker than ever. I'd learned of more shadows in the background, but all I really knew for sure was that a number of people were afraid, and that I was getting sucked into a giant mess. Same old stuff for me.

I needed a change of perspective, so I called my large friend Theo and invited him to dinner at a nice Italian place. Out in public, people tended to stare because of Theo's size and his dark skin tone, unusual for most of Maine. A lot of them got nervous, especially if we laughed even a little too loud. We ignored them like we always did.

Theo had a glass of Merlot, and I had my usual soda water and lime. He eyed me from across the table. "What do you want?"

I put on an innocent face. "What do you mean?"

"You need me for something. What is it?"

"Can't I just invite you out because I enjoy your company?"

"You can, and you have. But now you want something."

As a contrary cuss, I was tempted to tell him he was wrong, but I needed some handle on who was pulling the strings. "Okay, busted. You've got some connections. Can you trace a phone number for me, find out who and where it came from?"

"I can, but why?"

"Someone paid off and scared off a family, and left a number in case anybody came asking around. So the people at the other end might be connected to a kidnapping I'm looking into. I don't want to call it yet and tip them off."

He raised his eyebrows. "Shit man, you in it again?"

"Up to my eyebrows. I even went to church."

He laughed. "And you didn't burst into flame?"

"No, in fact the preacher was a nice guy. Then I met a politician who maybe isn't so nice. Helen Schiller."

Theo almost spit out his mouthful of wine.

"You okay?"

He coughed a few times, earning us skittish glances from the surrounding diners. If he needed a Heimlich Maneuver from one of them, he'd be out of luck. When he'd recovered, he wiped his mouth with a napkin.

"I take it you've heard the name," I said.

"Oh, I got a history with those assholes. My company was hired as security for a big event. Their people show up, get one look at me, and next thing I know, I'm told to leave. My services were no longer required. Guess they weren't expecting a black man when they hired us."

"I heard she was backed by some white supremacists."

"Found that out after. Man, I'd love to put a stick in their bicycle spokes. You need some backup? No charge."

I thought about it. "Yeah, just maybe. Could be some mob-connected casino people in on the deal as well."

Theo laughed. "You do find the deepest piles of shit to jump into."

"I have to do something to distract me from Allison."

He turned serious. "How's she doing?"

"Not well. They won't even let me see her."

"Tough, man."

"The worst."

Our food arrived, and we left the bad news behind.

After dinner, I pondered my next move. When people in an investigation didn't want to talk to me, it made me more eager to question them, to find out what was so secret that they were reluctant to give it up. While I couldn't go rousting ordinary citizens on a continual basis, I could badger Mason Carter.

Even though it was Sunday, I called and found out Carter was still working. I wondered if he was transcribing his interview with the singing chicken. I started surveillance at the building where his scandal sheet rag was published and hung around for an hour until he came out. He drove downtown, found a place to park, and walked into Gritty McDuff's, a local brewpub. I was sure I was in for a long wait.

And so I was. Three boring hours later he came wobbling out, by himself, thank goodness. I followed him back to his car. He tried to unlock it with an unsteady hand.

"Let me help you with that," I said, snatching the keys from him. "You're in no shape to drive."

"Goddamn you," slurred Carter. "Goddamn you to hell."

"Is this about Schiller?"

He shook his head. "Goddamned Schiller. Wish I'd never heard of the bitch."

"Why's that?"

"Not gonna tell you shit."

"It would really be in your best interest."

"No fucking way. You wanna get me killed."

"Did somebody threaten you?"

"Not telling you. Gimme my keys."

"I'll even drive you home if you just talk to me a little."

"Can't."

"Why not?"

"Gimme my keys."

Having waited all those hours to talk to him, I had lost all patience for his coy bullshit. I spun him around, yanked his arm up behind his back, and marched him to the back of his car. I opened the trunk and shoved him in as he started to squawk. I slammed the trunk lid, muffling his yells.

This was kidnapping, pure and simple, another sign I was going off the rails. I justified it by saying to myself that we had such a history that few would believe him if he accused me.

I got behind the wheel and started the car, playing the radio loud to cover his noise. It was Dylan's "All Along the Watchtower." I wondered if the universe was sending me some sort of message.

A few minutes north of town took us to a spot where no one would hear us. When I popped the trunk, Carter was sobbing, hands over his face. He'd also pissed himself. Now I felt sorry. Did he have claustrophobia or something?

"You're fine. Get out."

He scrambled from his confinement and fell. "Please don't. I'll talk, I'll talk."

Without getting up, he took a bit to catch his breath and recover, wiping his nose on his sleeve. He finally got to his feet and sat against the open trunk.

"Why are you so afraid? Don't like tight spaces?"

He tried to focus on my face, and gave a bitter laugh. He seemed to be getting back to his old self, and his meltdown had burned off some, but not all, of the alcohol.

"You're a real fucking bastard, know that?"

"Yeah, yeah. I didn't want to do it this way, remember."

"Well, I'm gonna tell you, I really am. You like sticking your nose in, let's see how you do with them. They'll fuck you up. Serve you right."

"So tell me."

"Gonna tell you. You just see what happens."

"Who are you afraid of?"

"Lemme tell you. But I'm not responsible for what happens, unnerstan?" He held up a finger like an orchestra conductor. "I'm not responsible." The words were terribly mashed, and I was losing patience again.

"Fine."

He bobbed his head. "Okay. Helen Schiller. Killer Schiller. I gave her that name, know that?"

"So I heard. This was after she shot that guy, right?"

"Gunned the poor bastard down on her own front porch. Fucking execution. So I gave her that name. Started going after her, you know?"

I knew all too well. He'd gone after me in typical yellow-journalism fashion, with innuendo and hints, trying to connect the dots to tie me into drug rings and organized crime. I'd had to endure a lot of pain and suffering because of it.

"Found out a lot of shit on her. Lotta shit."

"Like how she took money from the casino people to change her stance on the bill?"

He tapped the side of his nose with a finger. "That's one. You knew that, huh?"

"Found out today. So do you have a direct link?"

"Oh, I got that, and more. Lots more."

"Tell me."

"You know I don't like you, but I don't wanna see you dead. You sell a lot of papers for us."

"Thanks. And you're welcome."

"You're always a smartass. But these people will beat that out of you. And then kill you."

"Who?"

"Schiller's friends."

"The casino people?"

He took a breath, and seemed to be a bit sharper now. "Them. And the others. She was nothing, you know, a backwoods ranter with a lot of talk of sin and how thou shalt not do anything which might be fun. Gambling was a major sin. She was doing all these speeches against it, but wasn't getting out of her little circle. Her shooting the guy and then her pitiful run for governor should have been the end. All of a sudden she sees the light and changes her tune, talking about how a big business like that will bring in money and jobs for the hard-working common folk. And then she's floating on a sea of money and new influence. Got a state office and got a taste of the big time. And we start seeing out-of-state goons coming in, wanting to dip their beak."

"You talking organized crime?"

"Yeah. Boston mob wanted a piece of the action. And worse than that."

"What's worse?"

"White supremacists. They've got a clubhouse in Augusta, and a chop shop where they sell drugs, just up the road from that shiny new church. The church is now one of her recruiting stations. She was always talking shit against the impure races. When the Somalis started moving into the Lewiston area, she made a crusade against them. That got her some mileage. The redneck dipshits who've lived all their lives on public assistance started mouthing off about lazy foreigners. Things got ugly, and she had the muscle to push her agenda. The fringe groups came out from under their rocks, had some heavy hitters. Guys who cook meth back in the woods. Anybody who got in the way got squashed."

I took a guess. "Like you?"

He was quiet for a spell, and I didn't say anything. Now I'd let him take his own time. Finally, he spoke, his voice low and crushed.

"Got a cigarette?"

"No."

"There's some in the glove box."

Though I suspected a trick, I retrieved his butts, and a lighter that was with them. He shook out a cancer stick without offering me one and lit up. When he'd taken a good long drag, he started in.

"I was going after her, doing article after article. The paper got calls, threats, but we always get those. They started getting personal, but I was on a roll. Then one night, someone slipped a black sack over my head, and someone else punched me in the stomach." He paused. "They worked me over pretty good. They were wearing steel-toed boots." He wiped his mouth. "They drove me out in the woods and dumped me out. They took the bag off.

"Three guys, mean-looking motherfuckers. One with long hair, and two bald. One had a goatee. Fucking tattoos everywhere. They didn't even bother wearing masks, so I thought for sure they were going to kill me. One of the bald guys tossed a spade next to me and told me to start digging. I lost it."

The pity I felt for someone I despised was something I stowed away to examine later, see if it meant anything.

"So I dug, blubbering like a baby, begging them. They laughed, the rotten fucks. When they said that was enough, the one with the goatee took out a pistol. He knelt down and put the muzzle against my temple. '*This is what happens to nosy fucks.*' He pulled the trigger, and I heard it click. He laughed and smacked me up side the head with the gun. '*Next time you'll dig a little deeper, and you won't leave. Then we'll go after your sister and her kids.*' The bastards got in their vehicle and took off, spraying me with gravel."

He'd finished his tale and the silence lingered with razored edges.

I knew the answer, but I had to ask. "Did you see the license plate?"

He shook his head.

"Could you identify them in a lineup?"

"Like I ever would. Those fuckers would kill me, and come after my family. You know that. Look at the asshole you got put away, and they cut him loose."

The reminder of what had happened with Ollie Southern hit me hard. He was the reason Allison was in that rehab place, which was why I was so messed up. I blamed him, though I know there was a lot more to it. But I understood completely what Carter had gone through.

"What happened after?"

He was quiet again. "The next day, an envelope came for me at work. There was five hundred dollars in it, and a note. '*You like casinos now. Write about it.*' I didn't know what to do. If I didn't, they'd have come back. So I wrote a piece about how a casino would be good for Maine, and the following week I got another envelope with another five bills, and a note. '*Keep up the good work and stay healthy.*' I had to keep going. They'd have killed me otherwise. I don't know how to get out."

Carter had written a lot of shit for money, but this was a hell of a curse to be hit with. Even if he'd liked the money, it represented the fact that he was in thrall to killers who would scrub him at the first sign of disobedience.

I realized something else. I knew why he had told me. There was no love lost between us, but if I got involved, I just might get these assholes off his back. So he'd taken a chance, in hopes of me messing them up and maybe taking them off the board.

Of course, it would probably wind up getting me killed, and I was sure Carter wouldn't even be too unhappy about that, whatever his protests to the contrary.

CHAPTER 18

My psychiatrist was wearing a suit, not the casual attire I'd seen him in over the weekend. Maybe Monday was serious professional day.

"So you got into another fight? Since *Saturday*?" He looked at me over his glasses. Observant me could tell he didn't approve.

"Yes, but it wasn't my fault this time."

"And that makes a difference?"

I shrugged. "Just an excuse, right?"

"What do you think?"

"If I don't start it, I'm not to blame. I didn't know those guys would jump me, and I didn't hurt them."

He was silent. I knew this technique. He wanted me to keep talking, string myself out. Cops used this technique a lot, and I was used to it. But I'd said what I felt, and wasn't going to apologize for it. I crossed my arms and waited him out.

After another minute of quiet, he nodded. "Okay, that's how you roll. Is it working out?"

"Very little I do works out," I replied. "But I don't know any other way."

"You realize that a history of violence does not have to equal a future of the same, right?"

"You said to find something outside myself, some mission. One came along. I didn't ask for it, and now I can't shake it. But what I do means asking questions of people who don't want to give answers. Sometimes they react badly, and I just have to be ready for it."

He tapped his pen. "Think maybe you're an adrenaline junkie? You need this kind of danger to feel alive?"

"Probably. I heard a seagull cry on the way over here and wondered if it was an albatross."

"*Rime of the Ancient Mariner*," he said. "Got it. So you're under a curse for past transgressions?"

"Maybe."

"And you accept living with nightmares, ghosts, and flashbacks? Do you think you're making progress?"

I took a long, slow breath. "Hard to tell. All I want is for Allison to get better, and I'd even give up who I am to make that happen. I don't think she can live with who I am now. I want to get better, because every day is a struggle, and every night the ghosts come back. You said to focus on something else, so I did. Guess I'm not thinking of my own problems as much, so that's a plus. Haven't thought about drinking, either, so yeah, getting better. I'm talking to a lot of very scared people and somehow that makes me less scared. There's some dark shit going on, and I'm getting pulled into it."

"Are you saying your behavior can't be helped? Are you setting failure conditions?"

"Maybe. The only way I'm effective at what I do is by accepting the violence that comes along with it. There's a young woman missing, and some bad people are getting away with stuff by using fear and the threat of violence. When I enter the game, the playing field gets just a little more level."

He smiled. "Got a superhero complex?"

I laughed. "No, I wear my underwear on the inside, and I don't have a cape. But when someone's drowning, I'm not afraid of getting wet to try to save them."

"Well put. Seems to me you have this story you tell about yourself, and then you act it out. Whether the story is good or bad, you believe it. And that leads to many of your problems."

"It's the only story I know. It's not like I could be an accountant or something. Like Popeye, I am what I am."

He chuckled. "It worked for Popeye because he was a cartoon. You're a real person, and people who want healthy living don't get involved in fights and illegal activity on an almost daily basis."

I spread my hands. "You're right. It's unhealthy for me and those I care about. So tell me how to get away from everything that I am, while still trying to fight the good fight."

He shook his head. "You know the path you're on, and you know how to get off it."

"Yeah, I know the path I'm on." I sighed. "Look, I learned a long time ago there are wolves out there who will tear ordinary people apart without thinking twice. I was in with them so I know what they're like. Regular people don't have much of a defense against them. It's why flocks have sheepdogs who stand between the sheep and the ones who'd eat them. I'm on a mission now, looking for one of the lost sheep, and you said that would be good for me. But the only way I'm effective is to be what I am. That means busting some heads and taking risks. That's all I do. Hell, no one wants to talk to me about the crimes they commit. They just want me to go away. If I didn't go all out, I'd never have a chance of finding the reporter, and then I'd feel guilty about that. I have to try."

Sanders tapped his pen again. "You accept the danger, and you're willing to absorb the cost. If it wasn't so destructive, I'd almost admire it. Like St. George going out after the dragon."

I got up to leave. "Talking to you has helped me, Doc. A lot. But I won't be back, because if I change my life now, I won't be effective. I wish I could do better, I really do. But sometimes there *are* dragons out there and somebody's got to go fight them."

Dale T. Phillips

CHAPTER 19

Carter had told me of one of the white supremacist operations, a shop called Whiteline Auto Body. The place had an attached junkyard and wasn't far from the Church of the Redeemer. Owned by a pair of brothers, it was mostly a front for a chop shop, a place where they cut down stolen cars and sold them for parts. Carter said it was also well-known that they held dogfights and sold drugs and illegal weapons out of the place, and who knew what else. Bet they thought they were being clever with the name, which stood both for their racist stance and the fact that they sold drugs, a "white line" of powder.

The local cops didn't really have the resources to go after them, especially since witnesses were impossible to come by. People who dealt with them would be aware they had some heavy hitters behind them, and would kill anyone who ratted them out.

With leads being so scarce, I thought I'd check out this place. Carter had given me the info on their drug-buying code words, and I was prepared to go further down a dark road and make a buy. It would be my first time for that, though I'd seen others do it.

If you watch the places where bad guys do business long enough, you sometimes get lucky. Many crooks hate doing deals over the phone and are paranoid about the feds wiretapping them to get evidence of criminal activity. So they like the face-to-face contact. I liked to hang around and see what faces went together. Then I'd keep asking inconvenient questions until I turned up people who were lying or who had something to hide. I'd hang around long enough to make a nuisance of myself until some of the bad guys got nervous and tried to run me off. That gave me something to work with. It's like poking a bear with a stick until it riles up and comes after you. In that case, however, the bear was usually the innocent party. Here that wasn't likely.

The shop was down a side road and had a wire fence surrounding three buildings, with a junkyard behind. I parked off the main drag and hiked through the trees until I was at a spot across the road from them, concealed in a forest nook. I didn't want to get too close because guys who sold drugs and raised dogs for the fights usually had some dogs around as warning systems.

I made myself as comfy as possible, and got out my trusty binoculars. And then I spent the next four hours watching a whole lot of nothing. This is one of the drawbacks of surveillance; you need to spend many hours of absolute boredom in the hope of one nugget of something that will pay off.

They had a dog chained out front to a pole. It was a huge, ugly, brown brute with a mashed-in face fixed in a permanent snarl. Could give you nightmares. Anything I did with these clowns would have to take that dog into account, because I was sure it was trained to tear someone apart on command.

I didn't know if business was slow because it was daytime or just a Monday. It was past three in the afternoon when a red Toyota finally came down the road. I watched through my binoculars and almost dropped them when I saw the preacher's son, Bobby, get out. The dog was barking up a storm until one guy came out and smacked it, shouting for it to shut up.

The preacher's kid went inside the shop with the guy.

What was he there for? Drugs, most likely. Now, like Archimedes, I had a point where I could insert a lever and move the world. Or at least I could lift the stone to show the wriggling maggots beneath. It was enough.

The kid left five minutes later. I'd deal with him soon. Time for a little closer contact.

I made my way back to my car and drove down to the shop. I backed in to park, and left the door unlocked in case I had to leave in a hurry. Knowing my history, that was almost a given.

But I couldn't start out as an adversary because that wouldn't get me anything. I'd have to act like somebody interested in the more esoteric offerings of the shop. Carter had given me a couple of names to drop and as much background as he could. Give him his due, he'd acted like a real reporter for once and got some information on these creeps.

A man came out from one of the garage bays, wiping his hands on a rag. He looked to be in his late twenties and had long hair tied back in a ponytail. His dirty blue jeans were ripped, and he sported a T-shirt quoting the Second Amendment. He had tattoos on both arms, and more ink across one set of knuckles. "Something you're looking for?"

I smiled, knowing the code for heroin that they used. "Yeah, I got a blue 67 Chevy that needs a new fender. A man said I could get it done here."

He looked me up and down. "Maybe we can do that." Another man in a gray garage jumpsuit looked out from the bay. His head was shaved in skinhead style, and I could see part of a tattoo on his neck. One hand was out of sight on a rolling cart next to him. I figured he had a gun in there. Suspicious fellas.

"This man you talk to have a name?"

"Talbot," I replied. "Met him up in Augusta."

The two exchanged glances. The guy in the garage took his hand away from the cart and relaxed a notch.

"I might know him. What did he look like?"

I was glad I'd let Carter tell me as much as he knew. "About six-two, lean. Fiftyish. Black hair, glasses."

Ponytail nodded. "He say what our rates were?"

More code. "I told him I figured the repair would run about a thousand, and he said that wouldn't be a problem."

Dale T. Phillips

The two exchanged glances again. Ponytail licked his lips. "Mind lifting your shirt up?"

He wanted to know if I was wearing a wire to tape our conversation. I laughed and pulled up my shirt. Ponytail got a good look at the silver-dollar sunburst scar on my abdomen, like a bad appendectomy.

I let the shirt fall back down. "You like my prison souvenir?"

"From where?"

"California lockup. Only a few months, but it was enough."

He nodded. I'd passed the test, and I sure as hell didn't give off a cop vibe.

"Step into the office and we'll get your paperwork taken care of."

He led the way inside the first building, which had a counter separating an office space. The Confederate battle flag was hung on the wall, and I'd have bet money on there being a Nazi flag hung back in the shop somewhere.

Also on the wall was a calendar with a naked woman in a camo bandanna wielding what looked to be an UZI submachine gun. There was one chair on the customer side of the counter, and no magazines.

"We can't do all the repair today," Ponytail said. "Come by day after tomorrow, though, we should be able to fix you right up."

152

"I was under the impression I could get it done today," I said.

"Gotta get parts. Takes time for a big repair like that."

I said nothing.

"Got a down payment? Lets you see a sample of our work."

"Sure." I put a twenty-dollar bill on the counter, and Ponytail tucked it into his jeans. "Rafe, get our customer a Jackson package."

When Ponytail turned back, I asked him a question that I already knew the answer to. I was sure boys like these would have extensive rap sheets. "Do some time yourself?"

He nodded. "Couple of small things and two down in Thomaston." Thomaston was the state prison, so he'd made the big time.

The guy in overalls came back and handed his package to Ponytail, who put it on the counter. It was a small plastic bag and inside was a white powder. I tucked it in my pocket. "If this checks out, I'll be back for that repair."

Overall Guy was studying me in a way I didn't like. "I seen you somewhere."

"I don't think so."

"Yeah, on TV. Where was it?" He bit his thumb. "Shit, it was that trial. You was testifying."

Fame certainly came at a price. Ponytail reached for something under the counter and quickly stepped around to my side. I opened the door and moved fast toward my car. Ponytail came running after me. He swung a crescent wrench at my head. I sidestepped it, grabbed the arm that held the wrench and twisted. He yelped and dropped the tool as I bent his arm up behind his back. I got hold of his ponytail with the other hand and yanked his head back.

"Next time you try that, you better grease it first because it's going up your ass," I said.

"Who are you?"

"Triple A. We were checking out your repair shop."

Ponytail called out. "Rafe! Let Cujo loose."

I knew the Stephen King book, and my blood chilled at the thought of that mean-ass dog coming for me. I was only a few steps away from my car. I shoved Ponytail as hard as I could and sprinted for the car. Rafe unhooked the chain and a blur of motion burst forth, coming at me like a bullet. I got the door open and jumped in, slamming the door shut a microsecond before something large and hard smashed into the side of the car. I looked through the window at a huge mouthful of savage teeth. It looked to be about a hundred and fifty pounds of snarling hellhound. I started the car and peeled out before the dog smashed through the window and ate me.

Dale T. Phillips

CHAPTER 20

It was easy enough to find out where Bobby and the preacher lived. I drove up and saw the red Toyota parked in the drive, but no other vehicles.

I got out and walked over to look at the car. I squatted to inspect the paint job and soon discovered a fix on the left front fender, where it had been repaired, but not well.

"What do you think you're doing?"

Bobby was standing behind me, hands balled into fists at his side, frowning and red-faced.

"Checking over your car. Looks like you got some crappy work done somewhere."

"So what? What do you care?"

"Just wondered if your father knew."

"Who are you, anyway? What do you want?"

I took out the picture of Georgette. "See her around the church?"

He looked puzzled for a moment, but glanced at the photo. "Yeah, she came around a couple of times. So?"

"So she disappeared, and your church was one of the last places anybody saw her. So I'm wondering if anyone saw or heard anything. Did you?"

He crossed his arms. "Lester told me not to talk to you."

"Ah, and Lester is your boss, right?"

A flush suffused his face and throat. "I don't *have* to talk to you, whether Lester says or not."

"No, you don't." I tapped the fender. "Did you get this fixed at Whiteline Auto Body?"

The eyes showed fear now. "You better get out of here."

"Or you'll tell Lester?"

"I can tell the cops you're bothering us."

"Okay," I said. "Then we'll all have a nice chat about what else you get out at Whiteline."

He opened and closed his mouth, but no words came out.

"I got something there myself," I said. "I saw your car there, and they told me they sold you some, too. Just before I got there."

"They wouldn't."

"Why not? They're drug dealers, kid. They'd toss you over for anything. You're just a small-time customer to them, and they can always find more."

His brow was creased with lines of worry now. "What do you want?"

"Did you talk to this woman?"

"Yeah, she asked me some questions."

"About what?"

"Just making conversation, you know, about the church and all, and did I like the new place."

"Do you?"

He shrugged. "It's okay, I guess."

"Were you surprised when it was built? Like where the money came from?"

"Dad met a lot of new people who said they could help. They raised some money."

"Does Lester look like he wants to help?"

"What is it with you two, anyway?"

"You know what he is?"

"He's security for Miss Schiller."

"He's a white supremacist enforcer, too. Real bad apple. Like your buddies out at Whiteline. Does he know about your drug buys?"

The kid hung his head. Of course Lester knew. "So he said to keep your mouth shut, or he'd tell on you, or worse."

The kid nodded.

I sighed. "How'd you get involved with them, anyway?"

He looked at the car. "I was out with friends one night, and we were drinking. I hit something, messed up the fender. I didn't want dad to know. I'd seen the Whiteline tow truck around the church, and knew the place was nearby. I didn't know anything else about them. I just wanted to get my car fixed without dad finding out."

There was something else there that he didn't want to go into. "What about the drugs?"

He shook his head.

"Bobby, you have to tell me. I know they probably threatened you, but it's better if you tell me now, or things will get much worse for you and your dad."

His face screwed up like he might cry. "They said they'd fix it, and while I was there they offered me some pot. We had a joint, and it was good stuff."

"What else?"

He swallowed. "They told me they could sell me some, and other stuff, too, if I wanted it. They said I could make some good money, pay for the repairs, if I sold some at school."

"So you started dealing."

"Just some joints, I swear. I didn't want to touch the other stuff."

"So they got you in deep, and now own you."

"I don't want to do it anymore."

"I don't blame you. You don't think they'll let you quit, though, do you?"

"They scare me. They've got guns there. I've seen them."

I bit my lip. "I might know somebody who can help. It isn't going to be easy, but there might be a way to get you out, and keep you out of juvie."

"I'm eighteen. They'd try me as an adult, and I don't want to go to jail."

Back in Portland, I was having a quick conference with my attorney, Gordon Parker, who was a wonder. Not only was he the sharpest legal mind north of Boston, he was tall, immaculately groomed, well dressed, and had a full head of thick, flame-red hair. He mesmerized juries, and his rich baritone lulled judges and witnesses alike. Despite my prison record and constant habit of breaking the law and getting involved with criminals, he'd kept me out of jail so far. I paid him a king's ransom for his services, and he was worth it.

"And what trouble have you gotten yourself into now?" He leaned back in his chair and appraised me, probably toting up my bill for the equivalent of another year's Harvard tuition for his son.

"It's not me, it's for someone else. A kid, a teenager, who got mixed up with some drug dealers. They're also white supremacist gang members. They're too dangerous to cross without some protection. We could get him to testify, but we'd have to guarantee his safety, and his father's."

"What you're talking is federal witness protection," replied Parker. "But is there evidence of any federal laws being broken?"

"I don't know," I admitted. "Maybe enough drugs at the place to get the DEA involved? And they might have some guns, so maybe the ATF?"

"You know we can't work with maybes."

"Are you saying there's nothing we can do?"

"There's always something. Possibly I could work the racketeering angle for a RICO charge, if we show the connections. It's a tough sell, though. The feds like a rock-solid case."

"So we'd need to get something more."

"A lot more."

"Damnit. I can't do this right now. I'm already looking for a missing reporter, and time's running out. No matter what I do, someone's bound to get hurt."

Parker shook his head. "Sounds like you're in a world of shit. As usual."

Dale T. Phillips

CHAPTER 21

I drove out to the church to find the preacher and have a heart-to-heart chat about his son's future. They'd need some help to get out of the pickle the kid had put them in.

The preacher still wasn't there, but a woman in the church told me he'd be by around dinnertime, so I resolved to come back.

As I drove away, a dark, late-model Ford pulled out after me. It had a tinted windshield, so I couldn't see who was in it, but my spidey-senses were tingling. It looked like I had the reaction I wanted, even though I didn't know if it was casino goons or white power dirtballs. My money was on the former. Didn't matter, as I was ready to bust some heads. I was hoping they were here for the same. Either group was bad, and may have been behind taking Georgette, so I had an excuse for myself.

I didn't think we'd yet escalated to the "just shoot him" phase. Of course, I could be wrong. Still wouldn't matter, because then all my problems would be over. I was past caring, and once more needed the rush that violence gave me.

I drove at the speed limit, visualizing the road back to Portland and planning on a good spot to ambush them. There was a side road ahead, so maybe that would do.

A few miles down the road, I turned and sped down the side track before they'd reached me. I was around the corner and out of sight, and backed into a small cleared area among the trees. They came by a minute later, and were by me before they realized where I was. I pulled out, now behind them, and saw their brake lights go on. I guessed they were discussing what to do next.

They parked. So. A confrontation it would be. I parked, and got out at the same time as they did. One long-haired guy stepped from the driver's side, and a goon with a crewcut came out through the passenger door.

Big guys in suits. I liked that, as big guys didn't usually figure on needing guns against someone my size, and I was usually faster than muscle-bound gym rats. They had guns under their jackets, but they were probably thinking to rough me up a little, scare me off with a good warning and a beating. They were better dressed than Lester's other security flunkies and looked a bit more urbane. Late twenties or early thirties. Wearing sunglasses. If I had to guess what team they played for, my money would be on the casino goons.

"Howdy, boys," I called out. "You lost?"

The one with longer hair spoke. "You've been sticking your nose in where it doesn't belong." His accent sounded more Massachusetts than Maine.

"Nice dialog. What gangster film did you get that from?"

Longhair took off his sunglasses and set them on the top of his car. "Looks like we got us a real wiseass, Sonny."

"We don't much care for wiseasses," said crewcut. He took off his sunglasses and placed them on the car as well. They moved toward me.

I put my hands up, palms outward, and turned my body slightly, left side forward a bit. It looked like a placating gesture, but was actually a defensive stance. "Please, fellas, let's talk about this. I promise to be good."

"Too late," said Longhair.

With the blade of my left foot, I snapped a low, fast kick to his shin. He tried to pull back, but it caught him, and my left hand was moving as he reacted to the pain below. My speared fingers caught him high on the cheek and poked his eye. He cried out and fell back, even as his buddy drew into range. I shifted my balance and gave the second guy a kick to his shin with my right foot. I speared him in the throat and followed with a front cross-body kick to his now unprotected groin. He groaned and staggered back, clutching himself. I did a reverse spin and caught the first guy in the mid-section with a solid heel that took him down. I followed through and went after the second guy again, with a few well-placed blows that he couldn't stop. But he wouldn't go down, so I placed a foot behind his leg and used leverage to drop him. Too bad for him that his car was still in the way, because his head bounced off the back bumper. He wouldn't give me any more trouble.

The first guy was clawing inside his suit, so I had to pop him with a palm strike to his chin. I reached in where he'd been going, and pulled out a Sig Sauer pistol. I put that on the top of the car, and bent down and disarmed the second guy, who had a Glock. After a quick check for secondary weapons, I pulled their wallets and took out each driver's license.

Massachusetts, both of them. One with an address in Brockton, one from Quincy. Probably part of the Boston mob. I found something else in the wallets. Each had an embossed business card from Northern Mills Entertainment Enterprises, with a phone number, but no address.

These out-of-state enforcers preyed on others, them and their bosses. Once they came in, they poisoned everything with money. I needed to send a message that it wasn't going to be easy. These two would be my messengers. Looking them over, I felt the old anger start to rise. When that happened, things got extreme fast.

I dragged them away from the car and stripped them down to their jockey shorts, throwing the clothes inside their vehicle, along with their guns. I took their money and tossed the wallets in as well. I swept their sunglasses to the ground and smashed them for good measure. Using my Swiss Army knife, I punctured the gas tank on their car. I used an empty water bottle from my car to catch some of the dripping gasoline, and baptized the rest of the vehicle interior with several fill-ups. I made a trail of more gasoline leading away, and lit it. Blue fire raced in a line to the car, and soon after, the vehicle erupted into flame with a whoosh. As I watched the car burn, I wondered how much control I had left, as I could now add arson to my list of growing crimes.

I'd call the State Police and the Fire Department as soon as I got to a phone. These goons would be hard-pressed to explain what happened to the authorities, and then they'd have to go back to their employers and confess how they'd got their asses kicked by one unarmed guy. In their business, if you couldn't do the job you were sent for, you were in trouble.

Sweet dreams, boys, 'cause it's gonna suck when you wake up. Take that back to your employers.

CHAPTER 22

I came back to the church around dinnertime, and about twenty minutes later the preacher pulled up in his car. He seemed surprised to see me.

"Hello again," he said. "Good to see you back. What can I do for you?"

"We need to talk, Preacher."

"Are you in trouble?"

"Always. But so are you. And Bobby."

His face clouded. "Let's go sit down."

We went into the church to a spacious room in the back with a picture of Jesus on the wall, looking upward with soft eyes. We sat, and the preacher looked at me, his brow furrowed, his hands clasped on the desktop. "Tell me."

"What do you know about what Bobby's doing?"

He rubbed his face, looking worried, and suddenly ten years older. "You're talking drugs, right?"

I nodded.

He hung his head. "I was afraid of that. It's my fault. I haven't set a very good example, and haven't been a good father, either. It's why he turned to drugs and not the Lord."

"It's more that you've got these serpents around you, Preacher. You're in some really bad company."

"I know. Schiller and her people are pushing the casinos, and that's a sin. So I'm being punished for my support."

"There are worse people than the casino goons, although two of them came after me earlier today and tried to hurt me."

"What happened?" He looked at me, and concern showed on his features. All his troubles boiling around him, and he could still care about someone else. He gained quite a few points there.

"Things are spinning out of control. It didn't turn out so well for them. The woods can be a dangerous place if you're going after the wrong prey."

He studied me. "Does it have anything to do with the car that was set on fire? I heard about it on the radio coming back."

"The people who got Bobby in trouble are white supremacists. You're aware that they run an illegal chop shop up the road?"

"I've heard a few things. But Bobby's not a racist."

"No, but he banged up the car and didn't want to tell you. So he took it where he thought he could get it fixed quick and cheap without you knowing. But they're more than just auto body and repair; they're drug dealers. I confirmed that myself. They got Bobby to smoke some pot, and then convinced him to sell to the other kids at school."

The pain showed on his face. "No."

"Yes. And it does get worse. They're with Lester, security for Helen Schiller. You know him, but do you know what he is?"

"Some sort of criminal, I suppose."

"He's a white supremacist enforcer. And he's squeezing Bobby now, to help control you. And Bobby's afraid. I can't properly protect him. I've got a missing woman to find."

The preacher buried his face in his hands. When he looked up at me, there was genuine anguish written on his features. "And I let those people in."

"Why?"

"Because I failed. First, I was weak in matters of the flesh, like David, and took advantage of one of the young women in my flock. She became with child as a punishment, and everything fell apart. My wife died, and everything I'd ever worked for was crumbling away.

"I was approached by some people who said they could help. They paid the family of the girl to move away, and then they promised me this lovely new church and funds to keep it, and me, going. I thought it would be a new beginning for me and Bobby, and that we could put the past behind us. I thought we could help people. I confessed my sin and asked for forgiveness. That's what we're all about. But I made a deal with the devil."

"What part of your soul did they ask in return?"

"All of it. They want their temple of sin built nearby. I'd been against it, but now was forced to be their mouthpiece, telling people it would be a good thing."

"Well, now it's time to change the narrative, and redeem yourself in the process. They're dangerous people. Looks like casino mobsters have joined forces with the local white power groups."

He wrapped his arms around himself and rocked back and forth. "I don't know what to do."

"I do. We put a stop to them. We get you and Bobby into protective custody, and he testifies against these guys. You tell a grand jury what you know, and let the law do the rest. They'll clean out this nest of snakes."

"Will Bobby go to jail? He's eighteen, you know, legal age. I can't let that happen."

"I have the best attorney, who knows the system, and Bobby will not go to jail. He'll be a witness for the prosecution. You and he will get immunity. Believe me, the law wants these guys a lot more than they want you and your son."

"How do you know all this? Are you with the police?"

I laughed. "No."

"So how are you involved in all of this?"

"I started out looking for that reporter, the woman I showed you a picture of. Then I ran into a lot more. She's missing because she was after a story. Maybe it's something to do with all this. They certainly are capable of grabbing her."

He took a deep breath, as if an enormous weight was pressing him down. "They made me accept that Schiller woman and her people. Are they involved?"

"Lester is, for sure, like I said. Colby's a casino man."

"So I made all of this happen, because I was weak."

"Water under the bridge. Doesn't matter how it began. You have a chance to end it, do some good now. You can bring them to justice, atone for what you did."

He looked at me. "That won't be enough. My sins are too great."

"Wait until you go through the so-called justice system. Then you'll know what Hell really is."

"You make jokes, but I think you were sent to me."

I shook my head. "Preacher, I sure as Hell am no angel."

CHAPTER 23

I found an address for Northern Mills Entertainment Enterprises in downtown Portland. When I went there, though, it was just a mail drop. So I called Murrow and explained what I was looking for. He told me that there was a construction site with permits in the name of that company only fifteen miles from the church.

If they had taken Georgette, would they hold her at a construction site? It was out in the woods, so it was possible. I didn't know what I'd be in for, so I finally did something smart and called Theo. It would be much harder to jump me with him around. He wasn't working, and agreed to join me.

When he got in the car, I cleared my throat. "You carrying?"

"Yeah, but I thought you didn't like guns?"

"I don't, but after yesterday, they may decide to escalate." I gave him the rundown of what had occurred the day before.

He nodded, took out an automatic from a belt holster at the small of his back, released the magazine to check the load, and snapped it back in. "I get hazard pay for this?"

"I think the casino backers are bankrolling the white power assholes, who provide more local muscle."

"You're just trying to get me to work for free."

"Worth a shot," I said.

"So why are we sticking our heads in the lion's mouth?"

"Someone may be holding Georgette the reporter. A construction site is out of the way, so that's a possible."

Theo laughed. "You're trying to rile them up, too. How the hell have you been so reckless and stayed alive so far?"

"By having friends like you watch my back."

The corners of his mouth turned down. "How many you think might be out there?"

I gave him a look as I drove. "You worried about numbers? If all you've got is that little automatic, we'll probably be outgunned, too."

"Turn around. I can get more firepower."

"Nah." I gave him a toothy grin. "We've got the element of surprise."

"So we're outnumbered, outgunned, *and* outsmarted? Damn."

"That hurts."

"It was supposed to."

"Look, if it's any consolation, Maine doesn't have a lot of shootouts."

"I'm a black man going into the woods against rednecks with guns."

"Good point," I said. "So I should stay behind you, then."

"Asshole."

The site had a big Northern Mills sign, but I was more interested in the second sign, advertising the construction company of Richard Stone.

Theo looked at me. "Stone. Isn't that the dickwad you keep running up against?"

"Yeah. Figures if there's a dirty deal, he'd be involved. And now I know for sure what they're building here."

"Doesn't look like anything just yet."

"With Stone involved, I'll bet they're clearing the land for the casino."

"The legislature hasn't even approved the casino bill yet."

"These guys have been pouring in a lot of resources to make it happen," I said. "Guess they know which way the vote is going to go."

Theo shook his head. "Casino means mob. And all I've got is one pistol."

"You want to be Batman or Robin?"

"I want to be alive and go home after this is over."

I smiled at him. "You've got at least a fifty-fifty shot."

"We gonna do it, or are we just gonna sit here?"

"Saddle up," I said. I drove past a lot of heavy equipment, bulldozers, graders, backhoes, dump trucks, and more. Trees were being ripped up and men in hardhats were intent on tearing apart all the natural beauty of these woods. I stopped by a construction trailer, the only building in sight, apart from a pair of porta potties off to the side. I saw four cars and seven pickup trucks. One of the trucks had a Stone construction logo on the side.

"Maybe you should stay in the car," I said. "We don't want to scare them just yet."

"Gonna charm your way in, as usual?" Theo took out his pistol and held it by his thigh.

I walked up to the trailer and opened the door. Three men were examining something rolled out on a tabletop. Two of them wore hardhats, the third was overweight and in shirtsleeves. They all looked up at me.

"Howdy boys," I said. "Who's the bossman?"

Two of them looked at the one in shirtsleeves, who spoke first. "Who are you?"

"You work for Stone, or for Northern Mills?"

"I asked you a question."

"Zack Taylor. Who do you work for?"

"What the fuck are you doing here?"

"Sending a message to your employers. Which company was it again? I'm guessing these guys are with Stone, and you're the Northern Mills honcho, right?"

"You're not supposed to be here."

"It's all right," I waved my hand. "I've got special permission."

"From who?"

"Your bosses in Boston."

Shirtsleeves gave a startled glance at the other two. One of the hardhats was staring at me with a furrowed brow. "I know him from somewhere."

I smiled. "The physics program at Cal Tech, maybe?"

"Yeah," said the other hardhat. "I've seen him, too."

Shirtsleeves was getting red in the face. "You better start talking fast, buddy."

"Okay. Let's just say Northern Mills has worn out their welcome here. Time to move on before more than cars get burned."

"You." Shirtsleeves had his mouth hanging open. "You got some balls coming here. Sonny said he was going to find you and kill you."

"Well, that confirms who you work for. You might want to start looking for other employment."

"I know," one of the hardhats snapped his fingers. "He was on the news. That trial last year."

"Yeah, that's it," said the other hardhat. "Isn't he the one Mr. Stone is talking about? The big pain in the ass?"

"That's me," I said. "I already stopped one of Stone's casinos. Maybe he should try elsewhere."

Shirtsleeves shook his head. "I think this guy's here to get his ass kicked, what do you guys think?"

One of the hardhats smiled, a slice of pure nasty. "I'd say he came to the right place."

"Lotta woods out here to hide something, too, right? I'll call Sonny, and when he gets done with this asswipe, there won't be much left."

I put on a sad face. "If that's the way you feel, I guess I'll be going." I made a quick exit, and trotted on down to the car. As expected, they were right behind me.

Theo emerged from the car, and they skidded to a halt, just a few feet away. Theo had his arms crossed, but showing the pistol.

"Who the fuck are you?" Apparently, that was Shirtsleeves' standard question to anyone he wasn't expecting. He was panting like he'd just run a mile.

"I'm the big black bastard who's gonna start shooting if you don't get back up to that trailer. Knees first. Count of three, boys. One."

They scrambled back as if from a fire.

Theo looked at me. "Your charm had the usual effect, I see."

I smiled. "I swiped you a job application while I was in there. You can run a bulldozer and plow over trees. Won't that be fun?"

Theo made a sound of disgust and put his gun away. "No wonder everyone wants to kick your ass."

Dale T. Phillips

CHAPTER 24

I dropped Theo back in Portland. He waved off my offer of money, saying it had been a fun morning. I gassed up the car and headed south on I-95, down to Massachusetts. I had a stripper to track down.

Two hours later, I found the address in Worcester. The place was a seedy-looking motel that had seen better days. I spoke with the desk clerk, who for a ten-spot, told me which room to go to. I knocked on the second-floor door. The curtain moved in the window as someone peered out. The door opened, but the chain lock was on, so I had a view of a slice of a face. A man's face. Not a friendly one.

"What do ya want?"

"I'm with the agency. Here to see Carol." I figured I'd have much better odds of her talking to me with this lie.

He seemed unhappy that he didn't have an excuse to slam the door in my face. "Hold on." The door closed and the chain rattled. The door opened again, and the guy stood there eyeing me. He stood back to let me enter. He was about two inches taller than me, wearing pants and a wife-beater T-shirt that showed off his gym muscles, veins like a road map all up and down his arms. He glared at me like he wanted a challenge. With his gold chain, he was an easy target for mockery. But I had to tread carefully, because he looked like he would fly into a roid rage any second.

The blonde woman on the bed was wearing a kimono. She'd probably been a stunner five years ago or more but now she looked like she'd need low lighting and a lot of makeup to maintain the illusion of attractiveness.

She put down a magazine she'd been looking at. "The agency, huh? Good. I wanna file a complaint."

I took out a pocket notebook and a pen. "Okay. Give me the details."

She looked surprised, like she was expecting resistance. "Well, they told me to leave, with five days left on my contract. They gotta pay me."

"They tell you why?"

"I got allergies, and my nose was all red and shit. They said I was doin' coke, but I wasn't. It was just the allergies. I was takin' some medicine, and they thought it was somethin' else."

"Do you have the medicine with you?"

She looked startled. Wow. Hadn't expected that one, genius.

"No, I used it all. Haveta get some more."

"They gotta pay her," the guy broke in.

"And you are?" I looked at him, pen poised.

"Her manager."

Right. And overly jealous boyfriend as well. I turned back to Carol. "Did you try to explain things?"

"They didn't wanna listen. They just told me to go."

"Okay. I'll see what we can do."

"I should sue them. I will if they don't pay me." Her voice reminded me of a whiny child. "I got an agreement with you people. I make you a shitload of money, so you gotta stick up for me."

"Not up to me," I said. "One thing, though. There was a reporter?" I put the notebook down and showed her the picture.

She tensed up, not looking at the photo. "I never seen her. Don't know nothing about a reporter."

"So you didn't call her?"

"She already said that," Muscle-boy interjected.

I looked at Carol. "She disappeared right after she was at the club. So it's important we know what happened, and why she was there."

Muscle-boy couldn't stop himself. "What's this got to do with us?"

"An issue like this complicates things. Might hold up any potential payment."

Muscle-boy poked me in the chest with a finger. "There better not be any problems with her getting paid. We know some important people who can make a lot of trouble."

I was already tired of these two, and it came out before I could stop myself. "That why you're living the important life, in this shitty motel, whining about a few hundred bucks?"

He went goggle-eyed in disbelief, and reached to grab my lapels with both hands. I instantly slapped my hands over the backs of his, and bent down, keeping pressure on his wrist joints to force him forward into a crouch. I head-butted him, kneed him in the groin when he jerked back, and cracked him across the jaw with an elbow. But this guy was powerful, and not close to being done. He swung a punch at my head that would have split my face open, but I moved, and he hit the wall so hard it cracked the wall. He howled in pain, and I grabbed his wrist and elbow and jerked the arm up at a painful angle. Most people would have had enough, but he was still struggling. I spun him around and smacked the back of his head against the wall. He still wasn't down, so I did it again. Finally his eyes rolled up and he sank to the floor.

I turned to Carol, breathing hard. I needed her to talk before the idiot woke up. But she had too much to lose and so she wouldn't, unless she was scared. Really scared. I knew her type too well. So I had to bump up the lie. "I'm not with the agency. You know that now. But you've pissed off some very bad people, and you're in hot water. I don't care about you and your coke habit, but you better come clean about the reporter. The cops will be looking for her too, but you better tell us first."

"I don't..."

"Listen, you lie to me, you won't be dancing anymore, you got that? Do you need a lesson?"

Eyes wide, she shook her head no. A tear dribbled down one cheek, but it didn't stop me. I was sure it was fake.

"Now tell me about the reporter."

She looked afraid, and I didn't think she was faking that. "When they canned me, I was mad. I got her name from a newspaper, and called her. Told her there was some illegal shit going down at the club, she should check it out. I never even met her."

I let out my breath. "You called her for revenge, because you were pissed at the club? You hoped she'd find something, get them in trouble? That's it?"

"Yeah." Her voice sounded small. Now the tears looked real.

I was mad that I'd had to drive down here just to get assaulted and come up empty. But I really needed to save my real anger for the right people. Carol was the result of bad life choices, and even though I was the poster boy for that, I couldn't stop myself from a little lecture.

"You're off the hook for now. But clubs can't afford drug busts, and when you complain about them kicking you out for breaking their rules, you're going to be blacklisted. You won't have any clubs that'll let you work there."

I looked at Muscle-boy's body on the floor. "And take this idiot to the hospital when he wakes up. He's sure to have a concussion, even with that thick skull."

CHAPTER 25

Back in Portland, I called Theo and offered to buy him dinner in payment for his services that morning. An hour later we were at a downtown steakhouse.

He put down his menu, eyeing me with a suspicious glare. "You've got something else in mind. You're going to ask me to do something dangerous again."

I feigned an innocent demeanor. "Why do you say that?"

"Because this is the second time you're trying to bribe me with food. And I'm not a cheap date. And you have that look."

"Okay, maybe I do have something in mind."

"Thought so."

"I wanted to give you another shot. This time it's Schiller herself."

Theo perked up. "You've got my interest."

"On the drive back up, I was listening to that awful radio station that thinks she's God's sister. Turns out she has a political event tonight in Portland."

"And?"

"And I want to cause a ruckus."

"Why?"

"She's involved with some shady characters. They're scaring a lot of people. I want to shake the tree some more, see what falls out."

"Dude, you don't shake it. You head-butt every damn tree in the forest, hoping that reporter will fall out of one."

I shrugged. "Only way I l know of finding clues."

"You really are shit as an investigator. When you don't have any leads, you just start banging around." He grinned. "Still, this could be fun. Should I bring my gun again?"

I shook my head. "Bad idea. It's one thing out in the woods, but downtown is not the place for a shootout. They'll have media there, so it would be hard for them to kill us and get away with it."

"You think Schiller's behind the reporter's disappearance?"

"No idea. But when these people are rattled, they make mistakes."

After a fine dinner and time to digest, we walked over to the large hotel conference room where Schiller was hosting the event. She had finished her speech and was taking questions from the audience. Theo and I were out in the lobby, discussing our plan.

"You, my large friend, are the distraction." I said to him. "Show up at the door and burst in, make a lot noise. They'll come at you, trying to push you out of the room."

"Good luck with that," Theo responded.

"Just keep them occupied. Don't fight back or do anything to get arrested, but shout and holler, and maybe the TV cameras will record the struggle of the man trying to attend the open forum. Meanwhile, I'll slip in that side door and grab a microphone. I may ask an impertinent question or two. Then they'll come after me."

"I don't get to bust a few redneck heads?"

"Not tonight. But the way this is going, I wouldn't be surprised if you didn't get that chance at some point."

"Okay. Operation Big Loud Black Man commences in two minutes."

I peered in through the side door window. There was a line at the microphone, people queueing politely to ask their question of prospective Senator Schiller.

On cue, Theo swooped through the doors at the back of the hall, yelling that these people were racists. I watched Lester and three of his goons run to contain the situation.

I popped open the door and stepped inside. I moved fast to the mike, shouldering aside a tall, thin man with a receding hairline and a huge bow tie. He gasped in outrage, but I ignored him, speaking into the microphone.

"Ms. Schiller, would you care to comment on your contempt for true Christianity, since you take bribe money from a casino cartel to promote their bill in the legislature?"

There was a shocked silence, and I could almost hear everyone in the hall sucking in their breath. I went on. "How about your ties to the white supremacist movement? Any comment on that?"

Up at the podium, Schiller's face twisted into a grotesque mask of rage. Colby was beside her, his face white. The room erupted into pandemonium, and I handed the microphone to Bow-tie man amid the howls of outrage. "Your turn."

I booked it out of there, but wasn't fast enough. Lester caught up to me in the lobby, his arms reaching as if to strangle me, his goons behind him. I grabbed his outstretched arms, and spun the two of us in a dervish dance, letting him go after a complete revolution in a game of Snap the Whip. He flailed as he tumbled at the feet of the two pursuing security suits, and they all went down in a heap.

Once outside, I thought I was safe. Surely they wouldn't be stupid enough to continue the pursuit. But the outside door slammed open, and the two guards came after me.

So I took off running. I figured I could just outrace them, but where was the fun in that? I stopped suddenly, with a side kick that caught the first guy hard in the midsection. He stopped, and his buddy lunged for me. I dropped into a squat, catching him by the belt and the front of his shirt, and used his momentum to continue his path over my head and behind me. He arced and landed on his back in a pile of trash cans and garbage, splitting some open and causing a mess. I looked around, ready for the next attacker, if there was one, but the contest was over.

Now I was sure I'd get some kind of response to this provocation.

Dale T. Phillips

CHAPTER 26

My Treasury connection, Fielding, and I were eating breakfast at a diner. On the way over, I noticed a car that seemed too familiar shadowing me, but I figured I'd be safe enough for a meal with a government man with a badge and a gun. I'd deal with my followers later. Still, I sat where I could watch the entrance of the diner. I remembered how Wild Bill Hickok had ended, and didn't want to be caught like that.

"I'm surprised you agreed to meet me," I said.

"Well, you said you'd buy," he shrugged. "Plus, I admit I'm curious as to how badly you've screwed up all my latest investigations. I heard about your little stunt downtown last night."

I nodded. "I'm still looking for that reporter. I don't know if it's just wishful thinking, but I get a weird vibe that she's still alive somewhere."

"Who took her?"

"Not sure. There's so much going on, I can't put it all together."

He raised an eyebrow.

"Yeah," I admitted. "It's complex. Now I understand how hard it is for you to try to put all the pieces in place. You've only got so many resources, and there are a lot of lines to track down."

"And unlike you," Fielding said, "we have to follow rules. One slip-up, and everything goes down the shitter. Years of work, thousands of man-hours, millions of budget dollars."

"So this is me apologizing for saying you guys weren't doing your job well."

Fielding grunted and reached for the sugar canister to add more to his coffee.

"Here's what I know," I said. "All my cards on the table." I took a sip of coffee and pulled the condiment rack closer. I put a salt shaker between us. "This is the church. Preacher was against casinos, got into trouble. Trouble got bought off, he got a new church, and now he's a casino fan."

I put the pepper shaker beside the salt. "Helen Schiller. Anti-casino, going nowhere. Gets a new handler and a boost. Sudden money and power behind her, and *she* turns pro casino." I put a bottle of hot sauce beside the two shakers. "Helen's other new backers, white supremacists. One's her security chief. Dangerous muscle, squashes problems that get in the way. Like reporters."

I put the napkin dispenser at the side, overshadowing the smaller items. "The casino people, who are driving much of this. Neutralizing opponents, spending money and a lot of effort to remove roadblocks to putting up more gambling palaces. I was involved in one of those deals in Mill Springs, where the people running the town fiddled with the zoning so a developer could scarf up some Native American land for a casino. I was followed and threatened by a couple of armed goons, and I took this off them."

I set down the card for Northern Mills Entertainment. "You know it?"

Fielding nodded. "That's one of the front companies for the casino people. They sent muscle after you?"

"Yup. And I found out that there's a figure behind the scenes of all this, helping to make it all happen." I plunked the ketchup bottle in the middle of the array. "Richard Stone. He was behind the Mill Springs deal. He's on the board of Northern Mills. I went to a building site of his. Guess what they're clearing land for, out in the woods not far from the church and Schiller's backyard?"

Fielding smiled. "A casino."

I gave him a thumbs up. "Guess he's pretty sure of which way the vote is going to go."

"He should be. He spent enough to make it happen. If they get that place built, it'll be like the U.S. Mint. They'll be practically printing money."

"The on-site rep of Northern Mills admitted to knowing one of the guys that attacked me. And was willing to put me away for good."

Fielding shook his head. "You find out more in a week than my team turns up in a year."

"Because I don't have to follow the rules."

Fielding sighed. "And getting information here is worse than pulling teeth. These people don't talk much anyway, and nobody wants to help us, because we're the goddamned government that's never done a thing for them. The backwoods here remind me of the hollers back in Harlan County."

"How so?"

As he spoke, Fielding's professional mask slipped a little as his speech came more from his country heart. "Clans that stick together and do whatever the hell they want, because they don't give a shit about the outside world, and usually the feeling is mutual. But then somebody like the coal company or the casino people see there's money to be made out of the area, and swoop in, buy a couple of politicians, a preacher or two. Sometimes they turn people against each other, like those who want to sell versus those who don't. They rape the place, suck out all the money, and leave a shitpile, and the people wonder afterward why no one helped them."

I toyed with the sauce bottle. "Would you like to stick a thumb in their eye this time?"

"You know I would. But you get what I'm up against."

"Yeah. I'm only asking for a little information."

Fielding gave me a suspicious glare.

I went on. "If they're holding the reporter, it's someplace with twenty-four hours of their people around, but not near outsiders. I know some of their ratholes. The casino land site is a no-go. The headquarters in Augusta isn't right, because there's too much chance of being seen or heard. The chop shop out in the woods, possible, but I was out there and I doubt it. They've got to have a place in the area with one building or more that they likely use a lot. You've studied their financials, and the shell company buys of property and buildings. Ever come across anything that matches a place like that?"

Fielding wouldn't meet my eye. *Jackpot.* But would he tell me?

I stared him down. "What's the matter?"

"I can't."

"Why not? Another investigation?"

"Yeah. Goddamned FBI took it over. We found this place, told them about it when we heard what those guys were doing out there. Posted Private Property with a gate, one access road, no other way in. We did a flyover or two, and saw a few trailers, some storage containers. We hear they've got drugs, guns, probably more. But it's all rumors. Anybody that deals with them knows they'd be killed if they squealed. We've got nothing solid or provable. So no one can even get decent grounds for a damned warrant."

"So what's the FBI doing about it?"

"Sitting on their ass, like always. That was over a year ago. Hell, the bad guys might die of old age before anything happens."

I looked at him. "And you're scared of what the FBI might do to you?"

"I could get seriously fucked for interfering with their investigation. Prosecuted, even. No matter how slow or pointless it is."

"Even though you're the one who gave it to them?"

"That's how they work. They're like toddlers. Anything they touch, it's theirs forever, even if they don't want it anymore."

We were silent for a minute. I had to ask a man to lay his career and future on the line on a hunch. "Look, I know this could get bad for you if they find out. But if Georgette's alive, she may not be for long. They might decide to clean house, with the heat and all the people nosing in on them. I can take a run at the place, see if there's anything definitely worth going in for."

"Can't do it. Sorry."

My mouth tightened, and I was about to say something cutting, but I held back. He was from Harlan County, so he could be as mulishly stubborn as me. But he was brought up on pride and honor. I had to switch tactics.

I put a lone packet of artificial sweetener on the table and gathered the other items in around it, smothering it. "This is them. The whole bunch, with power, and money." I tapped the packet. "Want to know what they did to Mason Carter, for one? The first reporter? Three of them beat him up, bagged him, took him out in the woods, put a pistol to his head, and made him dig a grave. Makes me wonder about the other reporter. They steamroll people who can't fight back, just like the coal companies. In ones and twos, and ruin their lives. And they get away with it, because the people who could stop them bicker with each other. Look," I said, taking a breath. "Kidnapping is a federal rap. If I see anything to indicate the woman is there, or any trace of her, or any other things that would justify a raid, I'll call you, and you can bring the cavalry. FBI, ATF, DEA, Staties, every damn alphabet agency you got. Helicopters, cadaver and search dogs, SWAT teams. You get them ready. But you don't hear, you don't worry."

"Because you'll be dead. No way you're going to waltz in there and check things out and get out alive long enough to call."

"That's my worry. You know what happened out at Fort Williams?"

"Yeah, you took on a bunch of bad guys and kicked their ass. That's different. Injured goombah city boys are one thing, but these twitchy, meth-head rednecks are on their own turf, and they'll smell you coming a mile away."

"But they won't be expecting me, will they?"

He laughed. "Guess the hell not."

CHAPTER 27

I was careful exiting the diner, looking all around for the trouble I was sure was only a step away. When I got back to my car, Colby was standing by it, pushing up his black glasses.

"I don't like being followed," I said. "You could ask your buddies what happened when they tried it."

"Not my department," Colby said, his hands up in a placating gesture. "But I want to talk to you."

"I'm kind of busy," I said. "Got some things to check out."

"It's about the woman. The one you were asking about."

I stopped suddenly, fixing him with a stare. "You have my attention."

"There's a guy, says he has some information. But it comes with a price."

I let out a breath. "What?"

"He's been hearing about you from several quarters. He wants to meet you, talk face-to-face. And make you an offer."

"An offer of what?"

Colby bent and picked up a small gym bag, and tossed it to me. I unzipped it and saw wads of bills inside.

"Ten thousand," Colby said. "Cold hard cash. So you know we're not fucking around. That's yours, just to meet him and talk. You agree to our deal, you get a lot more than that."

"A deal?"

"You're causing us a lot of trouble. You know we want a casino, and that means jobs and prosperity for everyone. Negotiations are always delicate, because not everybody agrees. We don't like problems, and you keep showing up where you're not wanted and stirring things up. If this guy can tell you how to find the woman, you get off our backs, and you get a nice payday for your troubles."

"That's all I wanted, was to find her. I don't give a shit about you people and your casino."

"Then we're in agreement. Let's go."

I gave him a long look. This smelled as fishy as the wharf at low tide, but I had to run the play. It was stupid and reckless to go with him, but I couldn't help myself. It could turn out to be a legitimate shot at finding her. Maybe the casino people didn't like kidnapping, as it drew a lot of heat. So maybe they'd rat out the other team to get what they wanted, using me as an excuse, and get rid of two problems at once. Made a sort of sense.

I stashed the bag in the trunk and got behind the wheel, unlocking the passenger side door so he could get in. "Where to?"

"Near our building site where you caused more trouble."

"I thought I might make you people nervous."

"You got our attention, that's for sure."

We drove in silence for a bit. I was curious to see how much he'd talk. "How'd you get involved with Schiller?"

He looked at me for a long moment, as if debating, and gave a little shrug. "It's always useful to get someone powerful on your side. And she's going to be, thanks to us. But she wasn't going to do it by herself. I came on board to give her some polish, teach her how to talk to people, work with them. She'll stay bought."

"How much is she getting to sing your tune and be your dancing monkey?"

He laughed. "She gets to go to Washington, D.C. That's a pretty sweet ride, considering. I'm afraid you're not on the same pay scale, as you're a nuisance, not a help. But you'll be happy with the money. We can be generous to our friends."

"What about Lester? Is he your friend?"

I glanced over, and saw the corners of Colby's mouth turn down.

He cleared his throat. "Sometimes the people you do business with come with a little baggage. He's Helen's baggage."

So there was a bit of contention between the players. Good. "No love lost there?"

"Let's say our plans diverge. We want different things for the state. We're hoping that our way comes out on top, of course. Lester and his outside activities have become a liability. Your preacher friend has even demanded that Lester no longer step foot on church grounds. That got Lester worked up. He started mouthing off about how he was going to get even. Given that, and some other things, Lester will not be going to Washington. In fact, he won't be working for Ms. Schiller any longer. He's been let go."

"Hence this meeting?"

"Maybe."

"His people aren't going to be happy."

"Money fixes everything."

I looked at him again, trying to detect any sign of betrayal. Was he leading me into a trap? He didn't seem overly nervous, so maybe *he* at least was on the square. And he seemed certain I could be bought off.

"So how long have you known they had the woman?"

Colby turned his head toward me. "I don't know that at all. This guy says he knows something, but he didn't tell me what. It's for your ears only."

"Plausible deniability on your part, huh?"

"I'm just the messenger. I don't pull the strings."

"You pull Schiller's strings."

He waved a hand. "Look, I'm a consultant. We're business people, not a cartel."

"But you're doing business with some people acting like one."

"We don't always get to pick our partners."

I made a turn. "Actually, you do. You just choose the people and the acts you'll go along with. In this case, it's some pretty rotten apples."

He ignored my jibe. "You're going to want to make another turn up ahead. Take the left at the light."

I followed his instructions. "How about Stone? Where does he fit in?"

Another glance, and now he looked annoyed. "He's the land guy. You buy property around here, you deal with him. If he doesn't control it, he knows who does."

"Does he help out with things like getting a new church built?"

"That would likely fall under his jurisdiction."

"How about getting a trailer family to move to the coast into a nice house?"

"Okay," he said. "I get what you're doing. You put a few pieces together, and smell a good payday. So you want to know how much you can get out of us. I already told you, you'll be a happy camper, and you don't have to do anything else. It's easy money. But if you try to stick us for more, it's not going to go well."

"You guys on a budget?"

"We know what things are worth and what we want to pay. You're an added expense. Don't get greedy, though."

This guy was judging me by his own crooked standards. Probably saw the whole world the same way, through a green lens of money. He'd know the cost of everyone's soul, and the value of nothing. I felt a little sorry for him. "How much farther?"

"We're almost there," he said. I'd asked so that I'd notice if he tightened up when he said it, as he would if it was a trap. He didn't.

He directed me down a dirt road. My spidey-senses started tingling. There was no need for a meeting this far out, unless there was something else in play. Too easy to dispose of a body in these endless woods with no witnesses around to hear a shot.

He motioned for me to park. "Okay, we're here. It's just a short walk."

Now I knew something was up, even if he didn't. I got out and walked to the front of the car, and he joined me. I wondered if we were in somebody's gunsights even now. I guessed they'd want me further in, though.

"Down this way," he said, indicating a path.

I turned to Colby and punched him in the solar plexus. The air went out of him in an instant. I pulled off his Buddy Holly glasses and put them on. From the back of the car, I got out the Red Sox cap, and took out the sunglasses. I put them on Colby, who still hadn't got his breath back. I took off his jacket, and put mine on him. From a distance, if they didn't look too closely, maybe it would be enough to fool them. Enough to give me that extra second or two. Sometimes that was all you needed.

I pushed Colby ahead of me. His legs moved, his arms still holding his midsection. He still didn't have the wind to even ask me why. I kept prodding him forward.

We came to a clearing, and I figured this was the spot. If it was legit, I'd apologize, and we'd do our business. If not, well…

I gave Colby a little shove, and he took several steps out into the clearing. He raised an arm as if to hail whoever was out there.

A shot rang out, a crisp crack in the air, with an echo. Colby spun, and I saw his face and the look of utter astonishment. A crimson bloom sprouted from his chest. He fell, and I simply ran back down the path as if another hellhound was on my trail.

CHAPTER 28

I drove way too fast getting out of there, but I didn't know if they had a second shooter. I swerved the car every few seconds, in case someone was trying to draw a bead on me. All the while, Colby's shocked face haunted me. He'd believed his contact, that it was just a meeting and not an assassination. He was the Judas goat but instead became the sacrificial lamb. I felt bad for him, but not as much as if I'd been the one to get shot. I'd worry about survivor guilt later. If I survived.

Right now, I had to see to the preacher's safety. It was my fault for telling the preacher about Lester's connection to the guys selling his son drugs. Lester was one of those evil types who always have to get payback for every slight, every offense. No telling what he might do.

It wasn't far to the preacher's house, and I made it in record time, though my car would need some repair from the way I pushed it. I came to a stop in his yard with a screech of brakes, slammed it into Park, and jumped out.

Caleb came out the front door in a hurry, with a small suitcase in his hand. His face was tight, and his voice cracked when he spoke. "He's got Bobby."

"Damnit. I was coming to warn you. They fired him." I looked at the suitcase. "Ransom?"

He nodded. "He knew I'd been bribed to speak for the casino and Schiller, so he told me to bring that money. He blames me for getting him fired, but his people were selling Bobby drugs. I had to do something."

"Where are you meeting him?"

"Not far away, at a site with an old water tower and a pumphouse. If I give him this, he'll let Bobby go."

"No he won't," I said. "He'll just take the money and kill you both. You're witnesses."

"In that case, I'll be ready for him." The preacher pulled out a revolver. It looked like a .38.

I shook my head. "You think you've got it in you to shoot a man, Preacher?"

"If he's going to hurt my son, then yes, I'll put a bullet between his eyes while he begs God for mercy."

I looked in his face and believed him. Okay then.

"Right," I said. "You let me out just before we get there, and I'll work around and make sure Bobby's safe."

He shook his head. "He said to come alone. No cops, nobody."

"They always say that," I said. "But he won't know I'm there until it's too late. I didn't bring it up, but this ain't my first rodeo with bad guys."

"So it's true then, what they told me about you."

"We'll get into that later. Just understand that I've got a talent for this kind of thing."

He breathed out. "Okay."

"We'll get him back. Lester won't be expecting me. He might even think I'm dead by now. We'll talk on the way. Give me the money."

After I made an adjustment to the contents of the suitcase, we got in the preacher's car and peeled out. His driving was as reckless as mine had been just a few minutes before. We went over the plan, and he stopped on a side road.

"It's down that path," he said. "You'll see the tower."

"Okay," I said. "Give me a few minutes to get closer, see the setup. I'm hoping he's alone in this, which he probably is. His people won't be too happy with him right about now, but I want to make sure."

"Thank you," he said. His hands were gripping the wheel as if he'd tear it loose.

"Remember to breathe."

He nodded, and did so.

"And if you have to shoot, don't stop until the job's done. Go for the head, in case he's wearing a vest. Forget what you see in TV and in movies, some people don't stop with even a couple of bullets in them. Just end him, because if he gets a chance, he'll do the same for all of us."

I got out and jogged down the path, feeling a terrible sense of deja vu. For the second time that morning I was encountering a murderous, unseen assailant in the woods. I hoped that this time no one would get shot, but I had a sick feeling. Things were moving too fast for me to make good decisions.

I ducked off the trail and made my way through the underbrush. After several minutes, I heard the preacher's car coming down the path. There was a clearing up ahead, so I skirted further away from the trail, circling around. Through a break in the brush I spied Lester's car and the water tower, a rusted old thing. There was a metal ladder going up the side, and attached to it was Bobby, his head drooping down, one arm shackled to a rung at shoulder height. Lester stood beside him, watching the preacher enter the clearing.

A pump house was behind the tower, and maybe I could use that as cover to get closer. I watched for a minute to see if there was anyone else on Lester's side, but I couldn't tell, and there was no time. I'd have to chance it.

Keeping the pump house between me and where I'd last seen Lester, I ran and flattened myself against a wall. I took a quick look around the corner, and saw Lester with his back to me, talking to the preacher, who stood by his car. Good.

I crossed the distance between me and Bobby at the ladder, and then was beside him. He seemed drugged, and slumped against the ladder, getting orange stains of rust on his shirt. Luckily his wrist was attached with only a plastic zip tie, not a real handcuff. I got out my Swiss Army knife and cut the tie, and he collapsed into my arms.

I could see past my sudden burden to the two men squaring off now like an old Western.

The preacher gave a two-handed toss of the suitcase, and it landed at Lester's feet. When Lester looked down, the preacher reached behind his back. *Oh shit.*

Lester was more experienced, so his gun was out first. Two shots rang out, and the preacher dropped. I staggered under the weight of Bobby across my shoulders and took a few steps. Lester turned around and saw me. He raised his gun.

"Is the woman still alive?" Since I was about to die, I had to know if this whole journey had been for nothing.

He laughed, and the gun went down to his side. "The reporter? Yeah, we got the nosy bitch stashed. Schiller had some crackpot idea about turning her into one of the faithful, said God would change her heart. Won't matter now." He raised the gun again.

"You know Colby's dead," I called out, desperate for anything to stop the inevitable.

He shrugged. "Was supposed to be you. Again, doesn't matter."

"But there's no money in the suitcase. I told him not to."

Lester frowned. Keeping the gun trained on me, he knelt down and unzipped the suitcase enough to see the contents. His face flushed red as he stood up. "Where is it, you son-of-a-bitch?"

"I'll take you to where it is, but only after we drop Bobby someplace safe."

"I got a better idea. How about I start cutting off pieces of you and little Bobby until you tell me where it is?"

Before I could reply, a shot rang out, and then another, and another. Lester staggered a step or two and pitched forward, landing face down. I hefted Bobby and moved as quickly as I could to the car, and dumped him in the back seat. I ran to the preacher, who was bleeding in a dark red river.

His voice was weak and halting, fading away with his blood. "I got him, didn't I?"

"You did. Bobby's safe. Now you hold on."

"All done. What I deserve."

"Nah, don't talk like that. Bobby still needs you, so hang in there for him, alright?"

"'K."

I opened the trunk to see if there was any first-aid kit or anything to stanch the bleeding. All I could see were the piles of bills where I'd dumped the suitcase money out. I grabbed a stack and pressed it against the preacher's wound that was flowing worse than the other. I took his hand and pressed it against the bills. "Hold tight."

Picking him up with care, I maneuvered him into the passenger side of the car and propped him up as best I could, mumbling words of encouragement.

I hadn't really stopped to check if Lester was still alive. He didn't look like he was going anywhere, and I had two people to get help for. I started the car and stomped the gas. The car fishtailed a little as we swung around and headed back out.

But where to go? The hospital in Portland was too far, the preacher would never make it. I didn't know of any regional aid centers nearby. *Think, dammit.*

And then I got it. I remembered passing the station a mere five miles away. About four minutes later, I came to another screeching halt at the local fire station. I ran in yelling. "EMT! We got a gunshot wound. He's bleeding badly. Get an ambulance."

In seconds a guy followed me out with a kit bag. He did a quick triage and shouted instructions to two other firemen who'd come out to help. A minute later they'd removed the preacher from the car and placed him on a gurney. While they were all over him, one of the other firemen peered into the back of the car. "What about him?"

"He was drugged, kidnapped. Not sure what they gave him. That other guy's his father."

He reached in and scooped Bobby out. The guy was big, and seemed to have no trouble with the dead weight. As he walked away, holding Bobby, I got behind the wheel and started the car back up.

"Hey!" The big guy had turned back around to look at me. "You can't just go. We need some information."

"Something I have to do first," I said. "I'll be back."

I sure hoped I was right.

Dale T. Phillips

CHAPTER 29

Along the way, I stopped and called Theo. I needed backup again, and hoped he answered.

"Hey, man," he said. "I got a rundown of that number you gave me. Here's the address it came from." Theo read it off. It was the same address Fielding had given me for the property. Sonofabitch. I gave a short bark of laughter.

"What's so funny?"

"I'm on my way there right now, to see if they're keeping the reporter there. It's a white supremacist compound. They're armed, and I could sure use some help on this. Want to come?"

There was a brief pause, and then Theo's booming laugh came over the line. "Seriously?"

"I spent the last couple of hours watching three people get shot. Yeah, I'm goddamned serious."

"Okay then. Where do I meet you?"

Twenty minutes later, I did a drive-by of the place. There was a lone house with a dirt road alongside it that disappeared into the woods. A gate blocked the dirt track. Every other tree had a posted 'No Trespassing' sign. Seems they didn't like casual company.

I parked out of sight just up the road and waited for Theo, who came rolling up five minutes later. He got out of the car, all six-foot plus, the size of two normal people, and about as strong as any four. He held a Mossberg shotgun, and had a holster at his side with some kind of hand cannon that looked like it could double as light field artillery.

He saw me staring down the road. "What's the plan?"

"Thanks for coming. Uh, I don't have a plan yet, working on it."

He made a disgusted snort. "Same as always. You just charge in like a wild bull."

"Yeah, well, I've never done an assault on an armed compound before."

"So you have no idea?"

"There's a house down there at the head of a path with a gate. Fielding told me there was a gravel pit down just a ways, with a few trailers and some storage containers. At the house, there's a guy sitting on the porch out front. I'm guessing he's the sentinel. How about I go down there and engage him in conversation."

"Then what?"

"Give me five minutes, and drive by with your window down, so he gets a good look at you. That should shock him into something. I find a way to take him out, and we go from there."

Theo shook his head. "That's all you got?"

"You got a better plan?"

"Want me to wave the shotgun and yell something?"

"Knock yourself out."

A few minutes later, I parked and got out, hearing the low hum of insects, as well as a few birds off in the trees. The man sat in one of those bench swings on the wide front porch of the house, which faced the dirt track, instead of out toward the road, like you'd expect. Well, let's see what this guy was about. I trudged on up the slope to the house.

"How's it going?" I said when I got to the steps leading up to the porch.

"You lost? Saw you drive by before."

I climbed up to stand on the porch itself, and saw a cooler beside the man, and a can of cheap beer on a little table by the swing, along with a pack of cigarettes and a lighter. Pretty early in the day for a beer buzz. Next to him on the swing was a blanket, even though it was plenty warm enough without one. He looked to be in his late fifties, wearing a flannel shirt and dark green dickies, with white socks poking out of a pair of old worn slippers. He had an unremarkable face and thinning hair, but he looked at me through black-framed glasses. I remembered Colby, and felt ice run along my spine.

"Not quite," I said. "Looking for those fellas that live down that road."

"You are, huh?" He picked up his beer can and took a swig. "Now what business might you have with them?" He set down the beer and wiped his mouth with the back of his hand.

"Wanted to talk to them."

"They don't get any visitors, you know. Keep to themselves. Don't think they'd wanna talk to you."

"Is that so?" I looked at the road and back. "Known them a while, have you?"

"Can't say that I have."

This was all what I'd expected. "You've lived here some time, haven't you? Didn't move here from somewhere else?"

"Been in this house twenty-two years." He said it with pride, like sitting on this porch drinking cheap beer was some kind of noble achievement. Well, good for him.

"How long ago did they move in?"

He looked like he was thinking, but shook his head. "Oh, some time back. Can't rightly say."

"Why's that?"

"Eh?"

"You sit out here and watch, but you can't say when they moved in?"

He shrugged. Playing dumb. Okay, let's poke him a bit and see what he does. "What's the matter? That crappy-ass beer rot what little brain you've got left? You some senile old fart, sits out here pissing himself, because he's too stupid to do anything else?"

He stopped rocking the swing as his face changed. The bland mask had gone away, and a feral visage had taken its place, the eyes now dark and hard.

"You better get out of here. Now."

I laughed. "Why's that? You going to throw your beer at me?"

His face grew red. "You're trespassing. We take that serious up in these parts. And we got ways of dealing with problems ourselves."

"Pretty big talk from some dumb old goat with a cooler full of shitty beer."

He was almost hissing now. "You better leave while you still can."

I shifted tactics to confuse him. "Listen, old man. I got a big problem. There's an angry black man with a gun following me. I was told your boys down that road there could help me out, but you sit there like a fool and play games. I don't have time for that."

He frowned, trying to reassess what he'd just heard. I could almost see the wheels turning in his head. I knew what he was going to do when he reached under the blanket. He brought out his own shotgun and swung the barrel toward me. Pump action, and I didn't know if he had one shell ready to fire, or if he'd have to rack the slide first. Made a big difference if I was going to move. His feral face had a look of triumph. He had his gun now, and the upper hand. Big man.

"What you got to say for yourself now, smartass?"

I smiled. "I say you're committing a felony. Pretty strong reaction to me asking a few questions."

"You're not a cop. Who are you?"

"That's the question, isn't it? Who am I, and how many others know I came here? Who else is going to come looking for me? How long before someone comes down that road, asking questions? A lot of unwanted attention for you and most of all, your buddies down the road. Don't think they'll be very happy with you."

I saw the doubt flicker across his face. He licked his lips. Then his plan formed, and he smiled, a nasty little slash across his features.

"You wanted to talk to them? You're gonna get your wish."

"All right, then. We going to walk down, or take the car?"

"I'm gonna call them."

That was what I wanted to know, how they communicated. Now I was certain that he was their sentinel, watching the head of their access road and warning them of anything. Good. That made things easier. There was just the little problem of having a loaded shotgun aimed at me.

He stood up. At that moment, Theo finally drove by, hollering to beat the band, and waving the Mossberg out the window.

The guy went goggle-eyed. He was watching the path of Theo's car, and I moved, quickly knocking the gun barrel aside, so it didn't point at my midsection. He pulled the trigger, his eyes wide, but there was only a dull click. Dumbass hadn't racked the slide to load a shell.

I smacked him alongside the jaw with a palm strike, while holding the gun barrel. His eyes went glassy, and he teetered. I put both hands on the shotgun and ripped it from his grasp, and gave him a backfist to the mouth for good measure. He fell back against the outer wall. I tossed the shotgun onto the swing and grabbed his shirt with both hands. I slammed him against the wall, smacking his head in the process. He went limp.

"You and me are now going to have a little talk. Let's go inside."

I opened the door and shoved him through, leaving the door open. He was staring at the blood on his hand from where he'd touched his mouth. He looked at me with hate in his gaze. "I ain't telling you nothing."

There's a number of ways to get information. The most direct method is to cause the one being interrogated a lot of physical pain. I could get down to that if I needed to. But if he'd lived here a long time, he was attached to the place, and I could leverage that instead.

I ripped the front of his shirt open, sending the buttons flying. I spun him around and pulled the shirt down his arms to his elbows. I slammed him against the wall and yanked his pants down until they fell around his ankles. Then I hurled him back into a chair. His mouth was open in shock, but more importantly, he couldn't move much, entangled in his own clothes, and stunned for a few seconds. I stepped out through the still-open door and grabbed the lighter from the side table. I came back in as he was struggling to free himself.

"Don't bother," I said. "Or it'll get worse."

He glared at me, but stopped his efforts. From that position, he couldn't do much.

I pulled over another chair and sat in front of him. I held up the cheap disposable lighter and flicked it on. His eyes looked from my face to the flame, and he swallowed.

"Say you've been here twenty-two years?" I pursed my lips. "Arson is my new hobby. How long do you think it'll take for this place to burn?"

"You wouldn't dare," he croaked.

"Let's test that theory, shall we?" I leaned back and flicked the lighter on again, holding it to the bottom of a curtain.

"What are you doing?" His voice was high, cracking with disbelief. "Stop it!"

I ignored him. In seconds, the flame caught the material of the curtain and hungrily began licking its way up. I looked back at him, ignoring the fire behind me.

"You can tell me a few things, or we can watch this get bigger," I said. "Pretty soon, though, it'll be too late. Shame, though."

"You're fucking crazy," he yelled. "Put it out!"

"You going to answer my questions?"

"Yes! Yes! Put it out," he wailed.

I stood and ripped the curtain down from the top where the flame hadn't yet reached. I stomped it out before it spread. "Phew, that was close."

He looked like he wanted to cry. Which was the right frame of mind for questioning.

"Okay then," I said, sitting back down, holding the lighter in my right hand, where he could see it. "Let's begin. Tell me about your buddies down the road."

CHAPTER 30

The guy seemed convinced I was crazy, so he reluctantly confirmed that they had a captive woman down the road at the compound. One of the men there had said she was a reporter, that she'd been nosing around and got too close, so orders had come to grab her.

Theo came to the door and I let him in. I called Fielding's mobile phone and told him to bring the troops, but to give me a little time to get her out before storming the place, and wait for some sort of big signal. It would be stupid to have Georgette killed at the point of rescue.

Then I called Gordon Parker's office and left him a message about the preacher and the kid, that they'd need representation, and that I'd pay for it. I still had a good sum of liberated loot from a previous encounter. I gave Parker instructions on where I'd left them, and a quick-and-dirty recounting of what had happened. I also told him to prepare for a spirited defense for me, because I'd be breaking even more laws, and the feds didn't care what your motives were.

So I might be going back to prison, but I'd finally located Georgette. We needed to get her out. Besides, prison wouldn't matter if I didn't get out alive.

"What do we do with this dirtbag?" Theo prodded the glowering man with a big foot.

"See if you can find something to secure him with. Then let's put him in the trunk."

We looked around, and found some duct tape and a stack of zip ties. I wondered if the ties were standard equipment for this crew. We bound his hands and feet and took him out to the preacher's car. I opened the trunk, and saw the forgotten stack of preacher's ransom money I'd dumped out.

"Let's try your car," I said.

Theo was grinning and shaking his head. "You gonna tell me why you're driving around in a car that's not yours, with a pile of money in it?"

"It's a long story. How about we take care of things here first?"

We stuffed the guy in the trunk, with tape secured around his mouth so he couldn't yell for help. I took the tape and the rest of the zip ties.

Theo and I went down the trail through the woods behind the house, using the shortcut rather than the car path. The guy had told us about it, though I was sure there was a trap somewhere along the way. I took the lead, moving carefully and trying to make as little sound as possible. Theo was amazingly light on his feet and didn't crash through the forest like you'd expect from someone his size.

After a few hundred yards, I moved even more slowly. I sniffed, catching the scent of cigarette smoke. They had a sentry, but he was dumb enough to announce himself by smoking. Guess they hadn't had any real problems for some time and just got sloppy. Sneaking closer, I noticed the camouflaged blind by the trail, with the guy inside. Without the cigarette, I might not have noticed it before he saw me. I got right next to the blind without alerting him, and motioned Theo to come forward. He did, and the guy responded.

"What the fu—" was all he got out before I cold-cocked him and stripped him of the weapon he carried, an AR-15. Theo trussed him to a tree with the tape and the ties, and taped his mouth shut as well.

"Watch him," I whispered. "Anybody else comes along, do what ya gotta."

He nodded. "I'd say be careful, but I know you too well."

I gave him a nod and continued down the trail. It soon opened up, and I saw the layout of the place. It was a large gravel-and-sand pit, with two trailers to the left and one about a hundred yards away on the other side. A man exited from the trailer on the far side, wearing some kind of breathing mask. He pulled it off and sucked air.

There were three big metal shipping containers as well, and a little shack beside them. A woman with a long gun was in the shack, also smoking. I counted four pickups, two cars and motorcycles, and three all-terrain vehicles parked by one of the trailers. Through the windows of the two trailers, I counted heads as they moved. At least four, maybe more. Possibly more sentries out, too. Too many to take on, even with the well-armed Theo.

I got back to him. "There's at least six of them, probably others," I said. "We need some kind of big distraction."

"I could start shooting," he offered.

"They'd start shooting back right quick, and we'd never get out. Besides, I want something to get them to leave, not barricade themselves, so I can look around and find her."

We looked at each other for a minute. "Wait here," I said. I ran back up the trail.

Inside the house, I looked around and thought about the guy who lived here. He was rotten, part of the crew of criminals down the road. He'd known about Georgette, and that made me lose all sympathy for him. There was a pile of *Soldier of Fortune* magazines by the end table, and a gun rack that held pistols, rifles, and another shotgun. If he wanted to be a soldier for the cause, then I'd let him know what war was really all about.

I'd have my distraction, and a hell of a signal for Fielding to swoop in. I found a gas can in the garage, and brought it back in the house, sloshing it around the interior. Taking up the cheap lighter, I stood in the open doorway. I was wiping out an important part of a man's life, and I felt vaguely ashamed that it didn't bother me more.

Dale T. Phillips

CHAPTER 31

By the time I got back to Theo, I was out of breath, but there was no time to stop.

"Let's go," I said.

"What about the distraction?"

"In about a minute or two, they'll be distracted, all right."

We hoofed it down the trail, and stopped when we came to an overlook.

"I'm going to work my way down," I said. "When the shit hits the fan, I'll make my move. Anybody points a gun at me, shoot them."

Theo frowned and looked at his Mossberg. "Not at this range. Shoulda grabbed one of those rifles we saw. I could use that guy's Armalite."

"No time. It's about to go down. You any good with that hand cannon?"

He looked down at the pistol at his side. "Too much recoil for a good shot at this range. But maybe it'll scare 'em enough. It's a loud sumbitch."

"Make sure no one comes near you, or gets their sights on you."

"And don't you get shot."

"No guarantees," I said, and started working my way closer.

I was almost there when the shouts began. Men burst out of the trailer and pointed to the sky, yelling. The smoke from the house fire I'd set worked nicely, getting them all looking that way. Three of the men started up the ATVs, three more piled into a pickup, and they all roared off down the trail. The woman and another man stayed behind, both looking back toward the house. I came around one trailer and caught the guy from behind, pulling him back out of sight before the woman spotted us. I used a Judo sleeper hold on his neck that put him right out. A little longer, and he wouldn't wake up, but I told myself I wasn't a killer, even though there was evidence to the contrary. I took a quick look inside the trailer to make sure no one else was lingering, but the interior was empty.

I carefully crept over to the little shack, keeping the building between me and the woman standing out to look at the black smoke in the sky. She only sensed me when I was right behind her, and the barrel of her weapon spun around, but too late. I caught her under the chin with a palm strike that sent her into a backward fall, out cold. I took away her gun, unloaded it, and threw it into the brush.

Only one of the storage containers had a padlock on the outside, so I'd start with this one. I looked in the shack for a key, and saw none. I did a quick search of the unconscious woman, and she had a key on a loop around her neck. I pulled it off and tried it. Bingo.

The door creaked open, and light flooded the interior. I called into the dark at the back. "Georgette?"

"What now?" came a weak voice.

"Feel like being rescued?"

Silence for a moment, then the voice sounded a bit stronger than before. "Oh God, yes. Get me out of here, please."

"Can you walk?"

"Not well."

"Can I carry you?"

"Sure. Just don't get fresh."

I liked her a lot at that point. If she could go through that kind of captivity and keep her sense of humor, she might be all right.

"They're otherwise occupied, but we could still be in danger. So I'm going to rush us along."

She looked as bad as you'd imagine someone would after being locked in a dirty bin for days without shower facilities or anything but a chemical toilet that I saw off to the side. She was pretty ripe, too, but I didn't say anything as she tried to stagger to me. I scooped her up in my arms, and she felt so light. Too light. I guessed the feeding hadn't been overly generous. She felt like a baby bird fluttering against my chest.

I moved out, looking around to see if anyone had come back, or someone else had issued forth, but the compound was deserted of conscious people. I trotted to the front of the pit, and found Theo at the top.

"Take her," I said. She was already passed out. I picked up the shotgun when he took her in his arms.

"Christ, she weighs about fifty pounds. Didn't they feed her?"

We hoofed it back down the trail, passing our bound sentry, who still hadn't woken up. Close to the road, we heard all kinds of sirens, barking dogs, the crackle and roar of a burning house, and even a helicopter. The cavalry had arrived.

"Let's go back to the car, away from all this. We'll approach them from the road."

We got to Theo's car, and I popped the trunk, pulling out the frothing sentinel, whose cheeks blew in and out with the exertion of trying to speak. If I hadn't kept the duct tape on his mouth, he probably would have been roundly cursing us. I yanked him to his feet, but left him hobbled. Didn't want him running off. I put Theo's shotgun and pistol and holster in the trunk, as it would have been stupid to approach a bunch of frantic law enforcement people with guns in hand. They'd have likely shot us before finding out who we were.

We made an odd foursome walking down the side of the road. Just before we reached the site, a State policeman with a Smokey the Bear hat held up his hand as he frowned at us.

I looked him in the eye and spoke. "We need the Special Agent in Charge." I figured the FBI was probably on-site, and they liked to be the big dog in these things.

The Statie gave me a double take, but nodded. "Right this way, then."

The scene was a frenzy of activity, and at the center was a burning house being doused by hoses from two fire trucks. I saw a couple of guys in handcuffs, the ones from the pit.

The Statie took us to a suited man holding a walkie-talkie. He was yelling at someone. The guy was so frazzled, he'd even removed the sunglasses the FBI always had on.

"What?" He barked at the Statie, who indicated us.

The guy glared. "Who the fuck are you?"

"This is the woman they kidnapped. She's a reporter. They had her stashed away at the end of the trail. And this clown owns that burning house there. He was their sentinel."

The guy whose house was going up sank to his knees. The FBI agent frowned at us for a moment, unable to process. Fielding came jogging over. "This is the informant," he told the suit. The suit looked at him, and then back to us.

"She's going to need medical attention," I said.

The suit finally got it, and started snapping out orders. Two EMTs appeared, and took Georgette from Theo. Then the suit looked at the guy I'd bound up, and spoke to another suit who'd just come by.

"Get this guy loose, and then into some proper cuffs, and put him somewhere safe until I can get all this shit straightened out."

He looked at Theo. "He's the informant. Who are you?"

"He's with me," I said. "Protection."

"He looks like it. Anything you want to add to this shitpile?"

"There's a trail back of the house there that leads down to the pit. A sentry is bound up there, and there are two more at the end, if they haven't woken up and hightailed it out of there."

"Nah, we got them already, and the shitbags that came roaring up into our waiting arms. I'll send someone down the trail."

My throat was dry, and the smoke from the burning house wasn't helping much. "I could use a bottle of water, if you guys have one. It's been an interesting time."

The suit gave me a look that could melt iron. "We're going to have a nice long talk soon. Find a place out of the way and wait for me."

Once he'd gone away, I spoke to Theo. "I've got to make one more stop. Tell them I went off to take a leak or something."

Theo shook his head. "You mean you haven't caused enough trouble for one day?"

Dale T. Phillips

CHAPTER 32

This whole kidnapping and casino business mixed up with politics was a giant game of chess. A lot of the minor pieces had been captured, but the queen, Helen Schiller, was still on the board, powerful and deadly. The supporting props of Lester and Colby were gone, weakening her but not taking her out of the game. I didn't trust the law to bring her to justice, as I was far too familiar with the capricious nature of our judicial system. They'd sent me to prison for fighting back against a corrupt fed, while they'd released the killer Ollie Southern, even though he'd been caught red-handed while he and his crew were trying to murder me. And when he'd got out, he burned my business and tried to kill me again. He was the reason Allison had been so traumatized, and all because dangerous criminals too often aren't kept inside where they belong.

Schiller had money and connections, still backed by the casino mob. She was clever, ruthless, and manipulative. She'd get a team of lawyers to muddy the waters and throw suspicion on others. She'd wriggle out of it, maybe at worst with house arrest, probation, or a suspended sentence, but nowhere near as much as she should get. Then she'd rebuild her organization and keep everything going.

Me as the only witness wasn't going to do much good, as I was a prosecutor's nightmare. With my shady past, a good defense attorney could rip apart my credibility on the stand. Too much had been written about me in the papers, by Mason Carter and others of his ilk. So my only choice was to get something more on Helen Schiller, find some link to all that had happened.

Her house was shielded from the road by bushes and a fence, with trees on each side, and no other houses close by. The back was conservation land. A three-bedroom Colonial, it was still a modest house for someone with her money and power, all part of the image. Plain woman of the people, doesn't live so far above the common folk as to be out of touch. Smart move, because Maine has an attitude problem toward politicians who live in mansions.

There were no cars in the driveway, bolstering my hope that no one would be home. She wasn't married, and had no kids. If someone answered the door, I'd make up a story about being a meter reader or guy from the power company. I could usually come up with a quick and plausible lie. Not a great point in my favor as a character reference.

A front porch straddled the whole width of the house. I walked up the steps and rang the bell with my knuckle. No one came to the door, and I couldn't hear any noise from inside. I rang again, and still nothing. I tried the door, but it was locked, and I didn't want to break in unless I really had to.

I strolled around the place, though I doubted anyone was watching me. The back boasted a sun porch, so I walked up and tried the back door and all the windows that I could reach on this level. All locked. I stepped back down off the porch and studied the layout.

Running up along the side wall was a white latticework trellis, choked with ivy. From the top, I could get to the porch roof, and check those three back windows on the second floor. I gripped the slats of the trellis, giving it a good tug. It stayed firmly in place, secured to the wall. I pulled harder and shook it, and was happy to see it stayed put without too much wobble or give. I stuck a foot between crossed slats and put some weight on it. When it held, I boosted up, ready to jump down if I heard any cracking or felt it pulling away from the wall. The structure shuddered, but stayed in place.

Up I went, hands and feet finding purchase. Near the top, a slat cracked under my foot, but I scrambled onto the sun porch roof. The middle of the three windows wasn't locked. I saw no wires or alarm company stickers, so I used the heels of my hands to push the window up. It squeaked and required some effort, but went up enough to allow me to enter. I went in feet first, easing in and dropping inside.

It was a bathroom. There was a bowl of scented soaps on the vanity, and a crocheted tissue box cover. Various toiletry items were scattered around the sink. Only one toothbrush, a good sign that there probably wasn't anyone else but her living here. On the wall was a print of a foxhunt, the scarlet-jacketed riders caught in motion, their faces flushed with the thrill of chasing a defenseless animal.

I listened carefully, but heard nothing out of the ordinary, just a few ticks and murmurs of regular household appliances. It sure felt like no one was home, but I was nevertheless cautious.

I took out a bandanna to avoid leaving fingerprints, remembering I'd have to get the front and back doorknobs, and all the other places on the exterior I might have touched. I wiped down around the window and began my search.

One bedroom was set up as a home office, with a computer on the desk and papers in neat little piles. I took a quick look through the papers, but didn't see anything incriminating.

The master bedroom got a quick once-over. The closet held a floor safe. Too bad I hadn't learned any safe-cracking skills, as there was likely juicy stuff inside that could get her put away. Since I couldn't move it or open it, I left it there with regret.

There was nothing of note among the clothing in the dresser. The bedside end table, however, yielded a small .32 caliber automatic and a pair of handcuffs. I didn't know if the cuffs were for truly binding people, or for fun and games, but I stashed them into my pocket. I also emptied the bullets out of the gun and took that as well, vowing to dispose of it as soon as I got the chance. I liked to strip the bad guys of their weaponry every chance I got.

The upstairs sweep wasn't near as thorough as I wanted, but I moved downstairs anyway. The fridge and first-floor bathroom yielded no surprises. Likewise the other rooms, even though I opened drawers and cabinets and poked around.

Next came the cellar, but my quick look found not a speck of anything to tie her in with any illegal activity.

I sat on the couch in the living room, feeling frustrated and turning things over in my mind. Without any concrete evidence, things didn't look good for getting her sent away for a long stay. I took a last look around, and saw the hall closet by the front door. Inside, among the coats and sweaters and shoes and boots, was a double-barreled shotgun propped up in the corner.

A shotgun. Nothing illegal, but I remembered she'd killed a man on her porch with a weapon like that. Maybe it was the same one. Carter said it had been an execution. She'd blown away someone who'd crossed her, so if she thought I was standing between her and her freedom, maybe she'd try to do the same with me. With me out of the picture, she was a lock to keep out of jail.

The shotgun gave me an idea from an old Mickey Spillane novel. It was nasty, but I didn't have anything else. Using my bandanna, I took the shotgun from the closet. There was a cleaning kit on the top shelf, and I took that down as well. I broke the shotgun open and removed the shells from the side-by-side barrels. Turning the muzzle up, I took a piece of cleaning rag, wadded it up, and stuffed it down one barrel, packing it in with the brush rod from the kit. When I did the same to the other side, the gun was well plugged. I reloaded the shells and snapped the breech shut, then replaced the gun and kit in the closet. The shotgun was now a bomb for anyone who pulled the trigger, as the backed-up pressure would make it explode in the shooter's face.

I didn't want to think about what kind of monster this made me, but it would be worse to let Schiller go free to hurt and kill more people. Sometimes it takes a monster to stop a greater monster. That's why we had soldiers do terrible things in our name, right? We could sleep at night, as long as someone else did all the dirty work and paid the price.

With everything back in place, I opened the front door and set it to lock behind me when it closed. I stepped out and heard it click. I wiped down the doorknob, and did the same around the exterior of the house to any surface I'd touched. I put the pistol and the handcuffs in the car. Then I went back up onto the front porch and sat in a rocking chair.

She came by about five minutes later, and I saw her sitting in the car, watching me. She knew it was bad news, as I was supposed to be dead by now. She made up her mind and got out, striding up the walk.

"What are you doing here?" Her voice was smooth, under control. But I wanted her rattled.

"Waiting for you," I replied.

"What for?"

"To see your face when I tell you it's over. Colby is dead, Lester's dead, the setup is busted. The police have the boys from the gravel pit, and we rescued the reporter."

She chewed her lip. "Are the police on their way?"

"Just me for now. But I'll have a talk with them later today, and then they'll come. Looks like your run for office is over. Wonder how you'll look in a prison jumpsuit."

Emotions chased each other across her face, storm clouds in a murderous sky. I could sense the fury aching to burst forth, but she fought it down. Her face settled into something resembling composure, if you didn't count the twitches and the eyes glowing with pure hate. I saw something move in those eyes, and I knew she'd made her choice. I was a threat, and she didn't abide that.

She unlocked the front door and pushed it open. "Won't you come in?" *Spider to the fly.*

"No thanks, I can't stay. Just wanted to let you know how your plans are all ruined. We probably won't see much of each other after this, as you'll be in women's lockup, not down in Washington, D.C. like you planned."

I walked slowly down the steps, giving her time. The double click of the shotgun hammers cocking sounded behind me. I turned back. She stood at the top of the steps with the shotgun pointed at me, like some tough ranch woman from a western movie.

I put out my hands. "You think that's going to solve your problem?"

Hate wrenched her face into something gruesome to see, with blooms of red flushing her cheeks. She almost hissed. "It's going to solve the problem of *you*."

"You might want to rethink this. This is out-and-out cold-blooded murder."

She laughed, a bitter bark. "So? I've done it before, and he was standing right about where you are."

"Ah, planted the gun, huh? Police might get a little suspicious when it happens again."

"You going to tell me I can't get away with this? I'm going to be a fucking *senator*, you stupid son-of-a-bitch. Think you're so goddamned smart, like the rest of them. Figured out everything. Didn't figure on *this* though, did you?"

I shrugged. "I thought it was pretty much over."

"Not by a long shot."

"So tell me what story you'll be giving the cops about the second guy you killed on your porch, especially when they know he didn't like guns, and wouldn't carry one."

Her left eye twitched madly, but the gun remained steady. "You're not the first body we've dumped in the woods."

Guess I didn't know everything. "Don't you want to find out what I've got on you?"

"Not particularly. It'll be buried with you." She waggled the muzzle of the shotgun to the side a bit and brought it back. "Let's step around to the back."

"To make it easier to clean up the mess? Don't want my guts on your doorstep to show everybody? No, I don't think I'll go out back with you."

She grinned, a horrible thing to see, the flesh pulled back from her bared teeth. "Do it, or I'll shoot you in the balls. Take you a long time to die. You'll beg me to finish you off."

"That how it was with the other guy, the one you dumped in the woods? Who was he?"

"No one. Got in our way, that's all. Like you. I gutted him myself, just like a deer. He told me everything first, while he was crying and shitting himself."

"Did you get a sick thrill watching the poor bastard bleed out? Did he beg you, you murdering witch?"

"He did. Like you will. You and your big mouth. Now get around back, like I said, or I swear, you'll suffer."

"You do what you have to do," I said, and turned away.

I heard the blast, but didn't look back. She never even had time to scream. There was an eerie silence in the aftermath of the boom, as if the world itself was horrified at the deed.

I kept walking toward my car, trying hard not to throw up.

Dale T. Phillips

CHAPTER 33

The room of the police station had too many people in it, and everyone was in a suit but me and Theo. All men, too, so I knew the feds were still an old-boy network. I couldn't keep straight who was from which alphabet soup agency, but they were all looking to hang me out to dry. Treasury Agent Fielding wouldn't meet my eye, which was a bad sign. Our only beacon of hope was my red-haired attorney, Gordon Parker.

The FBI guy seemed to be running the show, but he had a short guy next to him with almost no hair left. That guy had a briefcase, so I figured he was some attorney. I wondered if my ass would be in that briefcase when he left. And there were other people listening in on the phone conference call, apparently from high up in the U.S. Attorney's office.

The FBI guy was explaining something. He was talking about me, and mentioning a number of statutes I'd broken, and which I could be prosecuted for, with chime-ins from the other agency guys. Though he left out about half, which I was grateful for, it sounded like I was the perp instead of the dirtbags who'd been arrested at the scene.

When the FBI guy stopped, it was Parker's turn. He was silent for a minute, all eyes on him. He took a deep breath, and began rolling out those rich, authoritative tones of his. It was like watching a great old Shakespearean actor play his favorite part.

"Gentlemen. You all are important men, with important departments to run. Here's the thing. My clients have given you, at great risk to themselves, a great, big ole Glory Cake. Every one of you gets a slice, and there's enough for everyone to share. You can all take credit for interagency cooperation in exposing and destroying a major criminal enterprise. You can all be heroes in this story. That way lies promotions and budget boosts next year, and great press clippings to pad your resume with. It's a win for everybody.

"But for some reason, some of you have got a bug up your ass about my clients, who are the real heroes. Furthermore, you're in a giant pissing contest with each other to see who can grab a bigger slice. This shit has got to stop, and you all have to get on the same page here.

"Bottom line? My clients don't like the limelight, won't talk out of school to reporters, and will let you all bask in your borrowed robes of glory, taking all the credit. If, and only if, you come to your senses as a group and offer full immunity over this engagement for all federal, state, and local offenses, and leave them the fuck alone after they testify. Am I clear? I hope so, because your precious jobs and fat pensions depend on it.

"Because anyone who decides to break ranks and charge my clients is going to fuck up the deal for everybody in this room, and the bureaus they work for. You will unleash a shitstorm of Biblical proportions. Not only will you spend the rest of your days in court, you will be crucified in the court of public opinion. Need I remind you it was a reporter, a good one, who was rescued? She knows who pulled her out of that crate, and he wasn't anybody with three letters on their jacket.

"The narrative at that point will be how your overly-funded, fuck-up agencies squabbled and pulled their dicks while a massive criminal organization ran free under their noses. How the top law enforcement officials had their heads up their asses and stood uselessly by, while two lone heroes were almost killed when forced to find justice on their own. Your Glory Cake will instead be the world's biggest Shit Cake, and you will eat every bite.

"Each of you is at least smart enough to know what your agencies do to scapegoats when the public demands blood. Bye-bye nice desk and cushy chair and a soft landing. Heads will roll, and budgets will be slashed. And I doubt any of you here would be in his position a year from now.

"Not all of you know me, but the ones who do will tell you I'm not blowing smoke. I will rain fire and death upon you and yours with so many suits you could start a men's clothing store, and the press and a battery of my fellow attorneys will burn your fucking houses to the ground.

"So make your choice, gentlemen. Either join hands and smile and celebrate a victory, or hit the unemployment line while the earth opens beneath you and swallows you whole. What's it going to be?"

There was a stunned silence. Men gave each other glances as if they couldn't believe what they'd just heard. The FBI guy began an objection. The phone crackled.

"Gary, shut the fuck up. Alex, clear Mr. Parker and his clients from the room. We're going to draft a statement."

Three of us were escorted out to the lobby, and I turned to Parker. "Nice speech."

He gave me a long look. "It better be. It's the only thing standing between you two and a small, barred room in a place far away."

Theo cleared his throat. "What do you think our chances are?"

Parker laughed. "These guys will cover their asses every time over doing anything else. They'll cave because they have to. They know I'm serious, so you two will walk, while they grab the headlines."

"Let 'em have them."

We had to be separately deposed, though, and that went on for a long time, while I made statements as to what I did or didn't know, and what I saw or didn't see. Yes, I'd seen Lester get shot, only after shooting the preacher. Why did I take off from the burning house and the crime scene? I had to see the preacher, and had stopped in to the hospital to see how he was doing. No, I couldn't account for the time difference. I told them I did stop for something to eat and drink, maybe that was it, since I figured I'd be tied up for a while. No, I couldn't produce any receipts for that time.

Of course, I didn't tell them about being at Schiller's, or how I'd removed and stowed all the ransom money from the trunk of the car. Nor did I tell them about Colby's death. I didn't know if he'd even be found, since the ones doing the shooting probably weren't too keen about having it publicized, and they'd had experience with body removal, judging from Schiller's comments.

After a very long while, we took a break, and I was outside, breathing in the air of a free man.

Fielding came up to stand next to me. "There's a lot you're not telling us, and they know it, but they also know they need you, and you're going to get away with it, you slippery bastard."

"They taking it all over from you?"

"No, like your attorney said, there's enough of a piece for everyone. Rescuing a kidnapped reporter and busting up a ring makes us all look good. In fact, they even made noises about interdepartmental cooperation, and are sending me some information that might be relevant to a case or two of mine."

"Will wonders never cease?"

"Like your buddy Richard Stone. We'll be paying him a non-friendly visit and microscopic audit in the very near future, I'm hoping."

"I'd like to see that."

"One damn time you might have actually helped me instead of screwing everything up."

"You're welcome."

"Don't be so smug. If it weren't for that expensive lawyer of yours, they'd have grilled you for lunch."

"That's why I pay him like a prince."

"Ever think about another line of work instead?"

"All the time."

Dale T. Phillips

CHAPTER 34

The hospital where Allison had worked reminded me of her and of my past sins that had landed me there for healing. This time it was someone else paying the price for the things I'd done. The preacher was a witness in an investigation, so they'd posted a uniformed cop outside the hospital room. I'd been cleared by Lieutenant McClaren of the Portland Police Department, so the uniform let me in.

"How ya doing, Preacher?"

He looked at me and smiled. "Bobby's safe, thanks to you."

"All your doing. Lester was about to shoot us."

"I did what you said. It worked."

"You okay?"

"I feel terrible about taking a human life, even if it was someone who deserved it."

"What about your wounds?"

"I'll heal, though it'll take some time. It's going to be rough."

"I've got the best attorney. I'll get him to represent you, take care of the legal problems."

"I'm less worried about that than about Bobby."

"I know someone else who can help with that. A good head doctor. He can get you two patched up, and help Bobby get off drugs."

"That's good of you, but I don't have that kind of money."

"Are you kidding? I've got a big pile of it from the ransom. You brought it, remember?"

"That's dirty money, tainted. A bribe from the casino people. I was weak, and I took it. But I won't touch it now. And it shouldn't go to the church, either. They've got a good fund of their own, from the same source."

"You're just going to walk away from it?"

"You keep it, if you want it. You earned it. From what I hear, you were like Samson in the temple, brought it all down on their heads."

"Well, I certainly have no scruples about taking it, if you don't want it. I'll use it to cover all your legal and medical costs, including the doctor I mentioned. They got you into this, so they should pay for all of it."

He thought about it, and nodded. "Fair enough."

I had some idea of what he'd probably been going through in his psyche, so I thought I'd give him a pep talk. "You're in the forgiveness business, right?"

"You want to be forgiven?"

"I was thinking of you, Preacher. You made mistakes, but now you know what it's like to be tempted and fall, and redeem yourself. That's what it's all about, isn't it? I think it's time you cut yourself a break from all that happened."

His eyes grew teary. "I've done terrible things."

I shook my head. "Not even close to what I've done. So if you can forgive me, you're way ahead in line."

"God's the one you should ask, not me."

"Like I told you before, God and me are not on speaking terms."

He smiled. "You're a good man, for a heathen."

I laughed. "I doubt that. But I try, every now and then. You take care of yourself. I've got another stop to make."

"Ah, yes, the reporter. It's been on the news. Quite impressive. You've had a busy few days."

I went to another floor to see Georgette. She also had a policeman outside her door, but my magic pass from McClaren got me in again.

Murrow was there, looking as if years had lifted from him. He gazed fondly at the young woman in the hospital bed, and I realized he was smitten with her. He'd always worship from afar, and bringing her back had probably saved his life as well.

She looked and smelled a lot better than when I'd pulled her from the storage bin. Apart from looking drawn, the only traces of her ordeal were some dark circles under her eyes, and a look in them every now and then that said she was remembering.

She gave me a sunny smile. Amazing she could, so soon after a tribulation like she'd gone through. She reached out a hand, so I took it. "Hey there, hero. I hear I have you to thank."

"It was Bob that did it," I said. "He never gave up, and got me on the trail."

"Bob, my other hero, do you want to formally introduce us?"

"Georgette Chappelle, meet Zack Taylor. A friend of my friend J.C."

"A pleasure," she said.

"Likewise. How are you doing?"

"A bit shaken up still, but otherwise okay. Glad to be eating and showering again. And to not have that nut job come by."

"Who?"

"Some dame who was driving me crazy. She'd come by and read Bible verses to me from the food slot at the doorway, and lecture me about sin and the true path of righteousness. I was looking for a way to stick something out through the slot and poke her in the eye, but never got the chance. I think she was trying to convert me or something."

I realized the woman was probably Schiller herself, trying to work her powers of persuasion, maybe as some kind of test. With the food and sensory deprivation, and having Georgette cut off from all others, it might have worked, given time. Then again, Georgette had proven herself to be one tough cookie. I liked her.

"And I've already got a book deal offer, can you believe it? I'm all over the TV, and apparently people in New York publishing saw this as the next big thing. I've been called with a bunch of offers, including talk of a Lifetime movie. They're quoting obscene amounts of money. God, if I'd only known the path to fame and fortune was to get kidnapped by dirtbags."

"But you're safe now," said Murrow.

I cleared my throat. "I hear that in situations of this nature, it's good to talk to a professional afterward, to help get through some of the issues."

Georgette pursed her lips. "You mean a psychiatrist."

"I was seeing someone very good. I think he might help."

Georgette raised an eyebrow. "You got kidnapped, too?"

I shook my head. "No, I was so depressed, I wanted to end it all. I was spiraling down fast. Bob here put me to finding you, and that saved me. So we saved each other, kiddo."

Her eyes were wet as she reached once again to take my hand. "I'll never forget what you did. Thank you, Zack."

"No worries. And I'll spring for the head doctor bill. You'll like him."

She smiled. "With what I'll be getting for this deal, I can afford him, but thank you. You've done enough. Maybe I'll even invite you on my yacht."

"Did they give any hint as to why they grabbed you?"

"I'm sure it was what I was discovering. Casino money, politics, and white supremacists. A lot of strange bedfellows were teaming up. I hear you threw a monkey wrench into the works."

"Called in the feds for the guys that grabbed you. They had enough other stuff down there that should keep the bad guys in the pokey for a long time. You helped break up a criminal enterprise."

Georgette turned to Murrow. "See? I *am* your best reporter."

"I never doubted it."

"Take care of yourself," I said.

Murrow took my hand on both of his. "I can never thank you enough."

I didn't know how to reply to that.

Dale T. Phillips

CHAPTER 35

Through the dayroom window of the rehab institute, I saw Allison working at her easel, applying brush strokes to a canvas and standing back to squint at the result. Off in her own corner, she was totally absorbed in her painting, ignoring everything that went on around her.

The doctor I was now talking to was much nicer and more sympathetic than the one I'd first encountered here. She bobbed her head to indicate the woman I loved painting away in the next room.

"As you can see, she's doing great. She's constantly working, producing a prodigious amount of art."

"So I can go in and see her now, right?"

A furrow creased her brow. "Let's talk in my office first."

I was impatient, but put it aside, and followed her down the corridor. A feeling of dread rose up within me. When they wanted to talk, it was never a good thing.

"Please, have a seat," she gestured to a chair. I sat.

"I have a few of her works here. I'd like you to look at them and tell me what you think."

"I'm no art critic."

"Please, indulge me." She took a stack of canvasses and set them next to the desk. She handed me the first one. There was Allison, and there was an image I recognized as me. Around me were swirls of darkness, spirals crackling with lighting and skulls, and scenes of death. Allison was in chains, reaching out to me, bleeding and bowed.

There were more like that one, and other images, canvas after canvas. I tried to remember where I'd seen work this personal and powerful, and then it came. The work of Frida Kahlo, after her accident, after the miscarriage, after the betrayals. These were depictions of internal pain splashed out for all the world to see, two dimensions becoming a chronicle of life. In them I was a magnet of death and darkness, Allison's torment personified.

My hands shook as I set down the last one.

"I think you understand," she said gently. "Much as she loves you, you bring too much pain and suffering with you. She cannot handle that agony right now, it tears at her. The expression of her inner turmoil seems to be helping. As long as she can paint, she can exorcise those demons."

My voice cracked a bit. "And as long as she and I aren't together."

"I doubt you're selfish enough to want to destroy her. But that's what being with her would now do. Perhaps in the future, we could change the associations, but right now, it's death and suffering."

"Are you saying I shouldn't even see her now?"

"She's making rapid progress at healing. We don't know how much she could slip back."

I tried to swallow, but couldn't. Everything I had and was since I'd come to Maine was in that room, unaware that I was only a few yards away. And better off for it. But for me, it was a death sentence.

"I'm terribly sorry," she said.

And so was I. There was nothing I could kick, or punch, or break that would bring her back now. She was lost to me. In a black daze, I wandered back out to the parking lot, where J.C. waited in the car.

"Sucks," he said. "I know a meeting we could go to."

"Screw that," I said. "You better find me another mission."

THE END

LIKE MORE ZACK TAYLOR?

Sign up for my newsletter to get discounts on upcoming titles
OR- Get a free ebook or audio book
At http://www.daletphillips.com

A DARKENED ROOM

While searching for a missing man, Zack Taylor stumbles across another body. Though it looks like a suicide, Zack isn't so sure, and he tampers with the crime scene in an effort to keep the police on the case. They do so, but from past history are suspicious of Zack's involvement. More than his freedom is at stake, though, because as bits of the dead man's activities become known, the danger mounts for Zack and the woman who hired him.

Read on for the first chapter of *A Darkened Room*, the sixth book of the Zack Taylor series.

CHAPTER 1

The dread that cut through me as I paddled toward the cabin was something I couldn't explain. I was not given to premonitions or glimpses of the future, or I'd have never done most of the terrible things that had caused my life to spiral into wreckage. I was simply looking for a missing man. Sure, I'd been told he was in some kind of mess, but none of the places I'd checked so far had given me this feeling of dread, a reactive spike of fear from deep in the lizard-brain.

I set the two-ended paddle crosswise and let the kayak drift silently. The morning fog coming off the lake was always a sight I enjoyed, so I didn't think my senses were reacting to that. It was the preternatural stillness, without even the calls of birds. There was no movement, no light from the cabin, no stove smoke of a wood fire, though the weather was cool enough to warrant it.

A smart man would have probably had the good sense to turn around and leave things as they were. The way I was wired, the urge to press on was a powerful itch, because getting involved in the problems of others kept me from drowning in my own.

And truth be told, I'd prepared for some sort of trouble. I'd taken the water route rather than the rough, rocky camp trail to the place. The Maine lake I was paddling on provided a handy place to ditch the latex gloves and lockpicks in my pocket if the need arose. The off-road vehicle with a kayak rack that I'd borrowed from my reporter friend J.C. was parked across the lake, the license plate smeared with mud to obscure the numbers. I wore an old ball-cap with a visor pulled low, a hooded sweatshirt, and faded jeans with L.L. Bean boots. There were a few others out this early: a canoer and two fishing boats, but I doubted that if pressed, anyone could provide a useful description of me. As a guy with a criminal record and all-too-frequent brushes with the police, I had to be extra careful when poking around. There were a lot of people on both sides of the law who would love to see me jammed up for any reason.

There was no dock or beach in front of the cabin to speak of, just rocks and a muddy flat, with a little grass and scrub growth stretching up from the water. I stepped out and pulled the kayak up, the noise of the bottom scraping on the earth a loud disturbance of the stillness. There was no place to tie the kayak off, so I got it far enough up where it wouldn't drift away.

The mud sucked at my boots. A few more steps, and I'd leave tracks if I kept going. At the edge of the scrub, I pulled out a couple of the plastic grocery bags I'd stuffed in the sweatshirt. These went on my feet like booties, and I tied them around my ankles. The latex gloves went on my hands.

I went up onto the small porch at the back. The solid knock I gave on the back door sounded loudly, and my call-out echoed from the mist. No response. I peered through the glass of the door top and the side windows, but it was dark inside, and I hadn't thought to bring a flashlight. There was one back in the vehicle, but I wasn't about to paddle over there for it. I did a complete circle around the cabin, noting the turned-over canoe off to the side, secured to a tree with a padlocked chain. There was a late-model Ford sedan parked out front. I peered in the windows of the car and tried the doors, but all were locked. In this neck of the Maine woods, people didn't usually lock their cars up. I thought about popping the trunk and searching the inside of the vehicle, but I'd check the cabin first.

The sun was struggling to overcome the morning mists as I went back to the porch facing the lake. I took out my picks and started working the lock, a talent I'd acquired from some people I'd worked with a long time ago. My skills were rudimentary at best, but this simple device was a cold cinch, and I cracked it in under a minute.

Inside the cabin I felt the damp chill that comes with being by the water, and I squinted through the gloom. Then the smell hit me, the stench of emptied bowels and death. My stomach lurched, and I forced myself to keep from throwing up. At that moment, a ray of sun poked through a hole in the shutter outside to illuminate the slumped body of a man sitting in a chair. The top of his head was so much shredded flesh, the filthy extinguished remains of a human life. I gulped again, and only kept down my breakfast by sheer effort of will.

I edged forward and saw the shotgun on the floor, a haunting reminder of more of my sins. Not long before, I'd plugged a shotgun that I was sure would be used in an attempt on my life, and the result was that an evil woman had blown her face off. Now this scene showed me a similar gory outcome, and I felt the guilt once more crushing me. I stood breathing in and out, trying to process everything. From the remains, I really couldn't tell if the body was Winslow Sprague, the man I'd been looking for, but I'd bet money it was.

When I could move again, I took a step and heard the floorboard creak beneath me. The sunlight showed more of the interior. Was this a simple suicide? Sprague had been in trouble, so had he taken the quick exit? There was no note, but that was no indication either way. The act itself was the dramatic final note of suicides, so many didn't feel the need to elaborate further.

I didn't like it. The reason I'd come to Maine in the first place some time ago was that my friend's death was thought a suicide, when it had been a murder staged to look that way. Police didn't investigate much on a closed case of self-inflicted death, and it shut down most of the questions. The death of Winslow Sprague would leave a lot of unanswered issues for me and for his daughter, and I didn't want it to end like this. Probably the psychiatrist I'd seen would have said my past influenced what I did next.

There was an easy way to keep the pot boiling. All you have to do is remove the death weapon, and the scene changes to look like a murder. And murders mean open, ongoing investigations. I carefully leaned down and picked up the shotgun, knowing I was committing a felony. I gave a final look around and slipped out the back door, locking it behind me.

I went back to the kayak, mud pulling at the bags on my feet. The shotgun and footwear went inside the kayak, and I stripped off the gloves and eased the craft back into shallow water and got in. I removed the bags from my feet and swished them around in the lake, then turned them inside out and balled them up. I pushed off against the bottom with an end of the paddle.

The mist was now gone, and I felt open and exposed. I stroked at a steady pace, sweat now popping out on my neck and shoulders and running down my back. Somewhere around the middle of the lake, I quickly slipped the shotgun out and pushed it into the water, letting it sink to the deep bottom. If the police were thorough and dragged the lake at all, they'd do it within throwing distance of the shore of the cabin, but they couldn't and wouldn't drag the whole lake. Unless someone had been eyeing me with binoculars in those few seconds, no one would know.

Back at the other side of the lake, I put on my socks and boots and donned a pair of sunglasses, further hiding my face. I racked the kayak and drove to the main road, then stopped and removed the mud from the license plate. Then I drove back to Portland, feeling a gripping dread all the way.

AFTERWORD

A Sharp Medicine is the fifth in the series about Zack Taylor, a man with many problems. He struggles to do better, but the deeds of his past weigh him down. When he tries to help others, he finds that doing good is a complicated matter, and unintended consequences force life-changing alterations.

He is more acquainted with death than most people. The ironic words of Raleigh indicate a man resigned to his Fate, but one who still will go out in style. Zack, though tempted yet again to give up, still clings to life in an effort to make a difference.

There is much to think about for those who wish to peel back the layers. If not, just enjoy a good action yarn.

Should you be startled at certain anachronisms, it's because this book is set in the 1990's.

This is a work of fiction, and any resemblance to actual persons, living or dead, is purely coincidental.

Dale T. Phillips

ABOUT THE AUTHOR

A lifelong student of mysteries, Maine, and the martial arts, Dale T. Phillips has combined all of these into *A Sharp Medicine*. His travels and background allow him to paint a compelling picture of Zack Taylor, a man with a mission, but one at odds with himself and his new environment.

A longtime follower of mystery fiction, the author has crafted a hero in the mold of Travis McGee, Doc Ford, and John Cain, a moral man at heart who finds himself faced with difficult choices in a dangerous world. But Maine is different from the mean, big-city streets of New York, Boston, or L.A., and Zack must learn quickly if he is to survive.

Dale studied writing with Stephen King, and has published novels, over 60 short stories, collections, as well as poetry, articles, and non-fiction. He has appeared on stage, television, and in an independent feature film, *Throg*. He has also appeared on *Jeopardy* losing in a spectacular fashion. He co-wrote and acted in *The Nine*, a short political satire film. He has traveled to all 50 states, Mexico, Canada, and through Europe.

Connect Online:
Website: http://www.daletphillips.com
Blog: http://daletphillips.blogspot.com/
Facebook:
https://www.facebook.com/DaleTPhillips/
Twitter: DalePhillips2

Try these other works by Dale T. Phillips

Shadow of the Wendigo (Supernatural Thriller)

The Zack Taylor Mystery Series
A Memory of Grief
A Fall From Grace
A Shadow on the Wall
A Certain Slant of Light

Story Collections
Fables and Fantasies (Fantasy)
More Fables and Fantasies (Fantasy)
Crooked Paths (Mystery/Crime)

More Crooked Paths (Mystery/Crime)
Strange Tales (Magic Realism, Paranormal)
Apocalypse Tango (Science Fiction)
Halls of Horror (Horror)
Jumble Sale (Mixed Genres)
The Big Book of Genre Stories (Different Genres)

Non-fiction Career Help
How to Improve Your Interviewing Skills

With Other Authors
Rogue Wave: Best New England Crime Stories 2015
Red Dawn: Best New England Crime Stories 2016
Windward: Best New England Crime Stories 2017
Insanity Tales
Insanity Tales II: The Sense of Fear

Sign up for my newsletter to get special offers
http://www.daletphillips.com

56928800R00163

Made in the USA
Middletown, DE
26 July 2019